Oh My God!
I Married A Devil

A Story of Triumph Over Domestic Violence

Oh My God! I Married A Devil
A Story of Triumph Over Domestic Violence

Copyright © 2013 By Diana Morris

This is a work of fiction. Names, characters, places, and incidents are products of the author's inspiration or are used fictitiously. Any resemblance to actual events, locales, or persons, living or dead, is entirely coincidental.

ISBN: 978-1-7334661-1-0
Printed in the United States of America
Fourth Edition

Dedication

This book is dedicated to my parents, Fannie Rabb Ringer and the late Sedric Rabb. Because of their love and support, I am able to reach my full potential.

Special thanks to my loving husband, Marion, and our four children, Micah, Jonathan, Marcus, and Malisa.

To my three sisters Debra, Betty, and the late Helen, your courage and strong will to continue to live past life's pain, inspires me every day.

Thank you, Dawn Mills Campbell and Joyce Scott for sharing your expertise and for motivating me to get this book published. God bless you both.

TABLE OF CONTENTS

Foreword

It is my honor to provide a foreword for this powerful, insightful, and noteworthy book. I am a 20-year veteran of the anti-domestic violence movement in South Carolina—the state that ranks number one in the country for men killing women. Diana Morris' book captures the degradation, worthlessness, and self-hatred that abused women have revealed to me during workshops and one-on-one sessions. Diana's central character is a Christian who, like many real-life women, tries to balance the Bible's template for a "good man" versus their human needs to have a man, even one with flaws. This character has to weigh and consider the feelings of her husband, her church family, and her own. *Oh my God! I married A Devil* is a realistic look at the ups and downs of a romantic relationship made even crazier when abuse rears its ugly head. The beauty of the book is that amid the doom and gloom, the book is seasoned with the sweet spices of HOPE, PEACE, RECONCILIATION, SELF-LOVE, and JOY.

In America one in every three women is abused. Simple math tells us that many of the women who will read this book will hear their own abused voices and see their own abused faces. Diana's book will help empower them to transition from victim to survivor. Hopefully, the male abusers who read the book will hear and see the damage they've inflicted and transition from abuser to healer.

As a playwright, author, and filmmaker, I'm aware of the power of artistic works. Oft-times plays, films, and novels are real-life occurrences with altered names, dates, and places. *Oh My God! I Married A Devil* is a novel but it's REAL, POWERFUL, EMPOWERING and a MUST-READ!!!

Eugene Washington

Eugene Washington is an accomplished playwright, author, and filmmaker. His work is always rooted in social/civic justice. Please visit his website at www.genewashingtonproductions.com.

Preface

At the age of 12, while sleeping quietly at home, I was awakened in the middle of the night by the sound of a telephone ring. As a child, I was scared when a call came in late because it usually meant something bad had occurred. After answering the phone, my mom and dad packed me up with my pajamas on, put me in the car, and raced over to my sister's apartment. I didn't know it at the time but my sister called my parents to say that she had just shot her abusive husband and father of her two young sons. I can still visualize the police officers at the apartment and the ambulance parked near the front door. Their children, both under five years old, were asleep and had little understanding of the fact that their mom had barricaded herself in their room. My sister's husband threatened to shoot her and the kids then drive to my parents' home and kill them before leaving town. Knowing the violent history of her marriage, my sister shot her husband during the altercation. He died on the scene. She was not charged with murder because the incident was proven to be self-defense.

I also recall as a teenager, fighting my boyfriend at a carwash while a male passerby yelled, "Take that to the house man". I thought to myself, "Why don't you help me? Can't you see he is beating me up? Why are you driving away?"

Should domestic violence be a private, take it to the house issue or should we shout it from the rooftops, "I am being abused and I need help!" According to the Centers for Disease Control, one in every four women will experience domestic violence in her lifetime and 1.3 million women are abused every year by an intimate partner. I am convinced that it is past time for communities, churches, and organizations to speak up and support those who are victims of domestic violence.

This book was written to inspire and encourage every person that has been affected by domestic violence. Despite the pain and suffering individuals may have observed or experienced related to domestic violence, this book will empower the reader to have hope and endurance and to continue to live and pursue a healthy, vibrant life. As the characters in this book will demonstrate, you are not alone. For those who have made a mistake or made the wrong choices, this book will demonstrate God's love and forgiveness, even if you feel you don't deserve it. Learn to forgive yourself and receive God's forgiveness. Never give up on love. And now abide faith, hope, love, these three; but the greatest of these is love. Love never fails (New King James Bible, 2012).

Oh My God!
I Married A Devil

A Story of Triumph Over Domestic Violence

Chapter 1
While I Wait

It did not take very long for Gina Mitchell to realize he wasn't the man for her either. Michael had dimmed the lights and put on a jazz CD, trying to set a romantic mood. He just knew that after three months of dating tonight was the night that he would finally hit a home run. After all, he was single, tall, dark, and handsome. He had a marketing degree and worked as the minister of music at one of the largest churches in Atlanta. Any sane woman would love to be in Gina's' shoes right about now. She really needs to know how blessed she is to be in her apartment alone with *the* Michael Wilson.

If Gina had not been one of the finest single women at the church, her name would be at the bottom of Michael's dating list. He walked over to the couch where Gina sat in a calf-length skirt with a modest split on the side. Her matching blouse was striped and buttoned nearly to the top. Gina was always taught not to show any more than necessary. If you show it all, they will want it all.

As the music played softly, Michael walked slowly to the couch and began to sing the words of the song with his deep bass voice. *It's you, baby. I need you.* He sat on the couch, leaving no space between them and gently grabbed Gina's hand. Michael's cologne fragranced the room and his clean masculine scent was breathtaking. Michael, wanting to be sure to take it slow, moved toward her arm and gently rubbed his hand from her shoulder to her fingertips then back up her arm and to the first button on her blouse. As Michael unbuttoned Gina's blouse, he leaned over and kissed her on the cheek, then on her neck. He paused, looked Gina in her eyes and went for an intimate kiss on the lips. Gina turned her head reluctantly and pushed him away.

"Stop, Michael," she said with her mouth. But her eyes were saying, "Wow that felt good!"

"Oh my goodness. Lord have mercy! Maybe a kiss wouldn't hurt," she thought. "No, I'd better not."

She got up from the couch, trying to compose herself. "Get a hold of yourself, girl," Gina said to herself. "This is not going to happen! Stand your ground. A kiss at this point for you is like pouring lighter fluid on an open flame! Okay, okay, you can do this Gina."

She took a deep breath, and, remembering her strict Pentecostal upbringing, she resisted the temptation to kiss Michael. She always wondered how it would feel to kiss someone that she really cared about. Now just wasn't the time to find out. She could tell by the lustful look in Michael's eyes that a kiss was only the beginning of what he had planned.

"Maybe it's the CD," he insisted. "I'll turn it off and just sing to you." He started to sing. His deep voice hit every note and modulation. *You are a special woman; a beautiful woman.* He gently held her hand and stepped closer to her. "Let's dance," he whispered. He gently pulled her close and snuggled his arms around her.

"Michael, I don't want to dance and you are too close. You're dancing like we're in the world. We are not in a club."

"Girl, dancing didn't start in the world it started in the church," Michael proclaimed. "Adam sang the first love song to Eve - *Flesh of my flesh, bone of my bone.* Don't you know your Bible?" he said, questioning her ability to rightly divide the Word.

"Yeah right," Gina replied smugly. "Adam said it but the Bible did not say he sang or danced and, if he did, that was his wife."

"Now I can give you some scriptures about singing and dancing but if you are not comfortable with dancing, I understand. But I do want to hold you close, Gina."

Michael continued to embrace Gina and massage her back.

"You are so soft," he whispered.

Gina was a virgin and had no idea the pleasure felt as a result of being caressed and touched by a man.

"So this is how it feels." She thought.

Gina felt as if she was going to fall to the floor. Immediately she thought of the scripture 1 Corinthians 7:1-2: *It is good for a man not to touch a woman. Nevertheless, to avoid fornication, let every man have his own wife, and let every woman have her own husband.* Gina's pastor had just taught at the singles conference last week that it is better to marry than to burn. Michael was there, too. But you sure couldn't tell by the way he was acting tonight.

"Look, Michael, I'm sorry but I cannot allow you to hold me like this or touch and kiss me like we are married. I made a promise to God that I would not have sex until I am married."

With a surprised look on his face, he rubbed his newly-faded haircut. The glossy waves were nicely tapered as if he had a haircut twice a week. The sweat on his forehead trickled down his face from the anticipation of being with Gina for the night. He wiped the sweat, pressed his lips together, and took a deep breath. He thought to himself and tried to build his own confidence. *Don't give up man. Stay focused. Your goal is to get her so relaxed that she will forget about everything but this moment and give in just like all the other women who have the philosophy of no sex until after marriage. If*

3

you say the right words and push the right buttons, even the holiest woman will say yes. Michael moved a little closer.

"You are beautiful, Gina. Baby, baby, come on now. You don't really believe in all that sex after marriage stuff do you? We can pretend we are married if you want to. You can be my wife and I will be your husband. Come on."

He pulled her close and wrapped his large hand around her petite waist. The closeness was almost breathtaking. Gina began to tremble even more. He sat her down on the couch and tried to reach for her button again. Gina prayed in her heart *Lord, if I am going to get out of this you are going to have to help me*. And, as if a rush of Holy Ghost power came on Gina, she pulled herself away again.

"Yes, I do believe in that sex after marriage stuff. So please take your hands off of me!"

"You see, that's why you are so mean. You need some loving woman," he demanded.

Michael was still not willing to take no for an answer. With his masculine biceps, he pulled Gina back snuggly into his arms.

"Now how do you expect a man to marry you when he doesn't know a thing about you?"

"Well if you are talking about sexually, then I guess he will have to walk by faith and not by sight because this is one car that will not be driven before purchased!"

Gina walked away from Michael toward the door of her apartment. She felt disappointed. *Lord, not another one*, she thought. She opened the door and politely asked Michael to leave.

"Michael, I am sorry but you have to go. I will see you at church Sunday."

"Oh, it's like that, huh?"

"Yes, it is. I will be praying for your soul, Michael. You need to go on a fast and stop being a hypocrite; directing the choir and being active in the church and knowing good and well that you are not right. You need to live what you preach brother."

"You can call me what you want, Gina, but you know you liked what was happening here tonight. Girl, you would be surprised to know all of the single people in the church that are having sex. I am a man, you know. God made me and he knows what he put in me. I have needs, Gina, and I don't have to get married to have those needs met. It would be nice to eventually get married but I ain't ready to settle down. I like my freedom. I like to travel and frankly, I would rather be alone."

"Well stay alone then and keep your hands to yourself. And another thing, about those needs you have, yes you are right; you do have needs. You need to be saved. You don't' think God knows what he put in you? He knows what's in you. That's why He gave you a way of escape, a way to flee fornication. Now here is the way to flee in this situation. Here you are in some frenzy of passion ready to get down. I have opened the door so you can run out of it and flee! So go! Do you get it? Use your self-control and leave!"

"Oh, so you're gonna play me like that, huh? Well, I am gone, Gina, literally gone. You don't have to worry about me calling you anymore either."

He repositioned his pants to be sure they were neat and buttoned his shirt.

"I wasted my time and money on you. You don't lead a man on like this and then leave him hanging."

"I did not lead you on Michael. Your flesh led you on. I will be praying for you."

Michael angrily walked out of the door.

"Man you are a trip! You must think you're gold or something."

Gina slammed the door behind him and spoke out loud in disbelief.

"God, I don't believe that. He was actually trying to take my clothes off. Lord, have mercy! Jesus, please send me my husband. I cannot take this anymore! Why is it so hard to find a good man - a man who cherishes me as a woman, respects my body, and does not lead me to sin against my body. Father, you said in I Corinthians 6:18 *Every sin that a man does is outside the body; but he that commits fornication sins against his own body.*"

Weeping loudly, Gina walked to her bedroom and began to pray.

"All I want to do is please you, God. The pressures of life are heavy. These temptations are getting harder and harder. I actually felt stimulated by that man's touch and I am sorry. Please forgive me. I'm sorry, Lord. I'm sorry, Lord. I do not want to become vulnerable. My flesh is weak and I had to get him out of here. Jesus, help me and deliver me from my own lust. I want to wait for the man you have for me. I hope for a loving, Christian husband, a man with similar goals and ambitions. It seems like these men that I meet are just Holy Ghost gigolos, full of games and no desire for commitment. Fornicators! I do not want to end up hurt or lost in sin. Lord, I believe you are a faithful God and you know my needs. Please send the right man for me. I need the perfect fit. I will wait on you, Lord. No matter how long it takes, I will wait to meet the husband you have for me; the man I am anointed to marry. But most of all I want to do your will, to please you in everything I do. Wherever my husband is, may he be blessed and encouraged in you."

Five hundred miles away, Bishop Anthony Smith, an honorable man of God, sat at the bedside of his wife, Kathy, who was dying from breast cancer. She was weak and deteriorating. Their short marriage of three years has been full of genuine love and ministry.

"You know, honey, when I'm gone I want you to remarry."

Bishop Smith gently placed his finger over her mouth.

"Sweetheart, please don't say that. I can't even think about another woman now. I am still believing God for a miracle."

"Honey, God has given us the miracle of our love. And as far as my healing is concerned, I have peace in my heart that God's will is for me to go home and be with Him."

Tears began to roll down Bishop's cheeks. His hazel brown eyes were hidden behind swollen eyelids. For months he prayed, fasted, and wept before the Lord on the behalf of his wife.

"Tony, God has heard your prayer and He changed the prognosis of three months to live. He has kept me alive for more than a year and we have made good use of our time. Haven't we? I enjoyed every moment with you, Tony."

She gently rubbed his head with her frail hands. She had been bedridden and not able to care for her personal needs for weeks. She looked at him with boldness.

"Tony, if I had my way, yes I would stay. But I know and you know that it's only a matter of time before death comes. I'm not afraid. I know that I will be with the Lord. And one day Jesus will say, 'Oh death, where is your sting and oh grave, where is your victory?' God's purpose for me in the earth is complete. I believe that it is my time to rest from my labor. I have fought worse things than cancer. My spiritual battles surpass this by far. I don't consider this a loss but again, I am going to be with the Lord and that is where

7

I long to be. But your purpose on Earth, Tony, is not yet fulfilled. You have to stand strong."

"Well, you are not dead yet. We can continue to pray. I speak life and not death. Life and death are in the power of the tongue. I refuse to hand you over without a fight. No weapon formed against us shall prosper and every tongue that rises up against us shall be condemned."

"Tony, we have prayed and prayed. We both know the answer to our prayers. Stop denying what you hear the Spirit saying. The Holy Ghost says not much longer. You are a prophet! You heard God and so did I."

She then pulled her frail body up in the bed and leaned back on her pillows.

"You know, Tony, I asked God to bless you with a wife that can help you complete the vision He has given you. With the last bit of strength I have in my body, I want to pray for you, my love, not for myself."

Tony began to cry loudly, thinking how lonely life would be without Kathy. He kneeled by her bedside and rested his head beside her.

"Shhh. It's okay, honey. You will be fine. I know you will. The Lord showed me that your biggest fear is that you won't make it without me. But you can, Tony. You can make it."

Kathy had been a prayer intercessor for many years. Her faith in God was phenomenal and her ministry was known internationally. The cancer had spread to Kathy's brain and spinal cord. For weeks she was unable to talk. Miraculously, today she could speak.

"Tony, I asked God to give me enough strength to pray for you and today, He has granted my request. This may be one of the

8

most important prayers I have ever prayed. I want more than anything for you to be what God created you to be. I see many souls that are in need and you must carry the gospel to them."

She placed her hand on Bishop's head and for the next few minutes, she prayed that God would lead and guide him to fulfill his destiny and lead him to the woman that would stand by his side. She concluded her prayer by declaring it is so. Later that evening the Lord took her home.

Meanwhile, Gina was still thinking of her encounter with Michael. She picked up the phone and called her best friend, Sheila, to fill her in on the details.

"Girl, guess who came over to my house earlier today?"

"I know! Don't tell me. Michael! You guys have been seeing each other a few months now. Is it serious?"

"Yes! Seriously over! He tried to have sex with me."

"No, Gina!"

"Yes and I should have called 911. It was just that bad."

"Yeah, I bet. Or the fire department to put out your flames," Sheila said laughing.

"Okay. Be funny, Shelia. This is serious. He was all over me. I asked him to leave. He finally left but he was so mad and I don't even care. Girl, that's why we have to pray. Everything that looks good is not good for you."

"Well, girl, we both will have to wait for a real saved man. I know God has some sheep somewhere but it just seems like all you and I have been dating are wolves pretending to be sheep. Do you remember that guy named Derrick who called himself a minister?"

"Yes, I remember."

"Girl, he was all up in the closet! He dated women for years and knew he was gay; gay as the word happy. When he came out of

9

the closet, the poor sister he married was devastated. She was just a cover up for his mess." Sheila said.

"Sheila, it is scary being single these days. You almost need a criminal background check before you date someone. And don't forget the HIV test. Statistics say that more women are contracting HIV now, even in the church. It happens in the church mainly because of ignorance. People just don't think it can happen to them. They just get married and don't even think about checking their HIV status. Now let's face it, some of these men already know they are HIV positive but they still come into the church and start dating these sisters. They fall in love, get married, and transmit the disease. Then, here comes the big confession after the fact. Girl, it is sad; truly sad. We are certainly living in the last and evil days. Can you imagine being virgins like us and getting married to someone who is HIV positive?"

"No, I cannot imagine it and I don't want to try," Sheila replied. "Maybe we should just stay single and forget about getting married."

"No girl! It's bad but it ain't that bad! I believe God is able to send me the right man that is not sick spiritually or physically. While I wait, I have decided to go back to college and finish my degree. I am tired of being an administrative assistant. I want to increase my knowledge and income."

"What will you major in?"

"I don't know yet. I will see what credits will transfer and all that stuff. I've thought about a health profession or something like that."

"Yes, healthcare is a good field. You would make a good nurse, Gina."

"Yeah right. I hate needles. So I know I will not be a nurse.

Gina's phone line beeped.

"Sheila, it's my mom. Let me chat with her for a minute. Are you going to church tomorrow night?"

"Yes. I heard that Prophet Joel is going to be the speaker so you know we have to get there early. The house is going to be packed. I think the young people's choir is supposed to sing and the praise team will open up as usual."

"Okay girl, I guess I will see you tomorrow. Good night."

Gina clicked over to the other line.

"Hello, Mama. What are you doing up so late?"

"Hi, baby. I was just checking in on you. I had a dream about you and I had to call you right away."

"Oh Lord, Mama. What was it about? Don't tell me you had collard greens and cornbread before you went to bed."

"No, honey. I am on a fast actually. Gina, you know me better than that. I don't like to just jump to saying that God gave me a dream but this was something that I think I should share with you. In my dream, you were surrounded by demons and they were talking to you and telling you things that I could not hear. All I could see was you wearing a long white wedding gown. You were happy and smiling. But you were walking toward a dark hole and there was a man inside the hole telling you to come with him. Your dad and I yelled your name and told you not to go in there but you smiled and told us not to worry; that you were fine. I woke up and I have been thinking about the dream ever since. I just couldn't go back to sleep. Is there something going on in your life?"

"Yes, Mama, as a matter of fact, it is. You know Michael, the guy I have been dating for a while? Well, he tried to have sex with me tonight. So that is probably what your dream was about but don't worry, I put him out and he won't be coming back."

11

"Well thank the Lord for that. I hope that was what the dream was about. The only thing I don't like is you were smiling and you did not know what was happening to you in the spirit realm. Stay prayerful, Gina, and be careful. You know we can't be ignorant to the devil's devices."

"Don't worry, Mom. I will. I pray three times a day and then some."

The next evening church service was on fire as the praise and worship went to a different level. Gina was deep into the praise.

"Hallelujah! Lord, prepare me to be a sanctuary. I want to be tried and true. I want to be used in your kingdom," she proclaimed with tears in her eyes.

After Bishop Joel preached, he began to operate in the prophetic gift and, during the altar call, he prophesied to Gina. "Dear sister, I see you completing college and working as an engineer. Are you a preacher? "

"No, I am not."

"Well, I also see you preaching the gospel. Continue fasting and praying that the Lord will reveal to you His plans for your life."

Gina mumbled to herself as she walked back to her seat.

"Engineering? Don't you have to be smart to be an engineer? And a preacher!" With unbelief in her mind, Gina said to herself, "Maybe he has me mixed up with someone else. I am just gonna have to pray about this."

Chapter 2

A Higher Calling

Two years later, Gina completed a degree in chemical engineering.

"Sheila, the Lord has blessed me to complete my degree and has given me favor to obtain a good paying job."

"I know. God is so good, Gina. I am happy for you. I don't know how you managed to study and stay on the choir with everything else you had on your plate. It had to be God."

"Yes nobody but Jesus! Well thanks for the dinner, Sheila. I will call you tomorrow. I need to get home tonight and spend some time in the Word."

"Okay. You are welcome. Good night."

Gina left Sheila's place and headed home. Once inside, she fell to her knees in prayer, thanking God for all of His blessings. During the prayer, the Lord spoke to Gina and called her to preach the gospel. Gina began to cry and pray in an unknown Heavenly language.

"Why me, God? I don't want to preach. Just let me sing. You have plenty of preachers."

The Lord responded, "I have chosen you to preach my Word. Now study to show yourself approved."

"Yes Lord."

To prepare for the ministry, Gina decided to attend Bible College where she studied hard and graduated at the top of her class. She earned a degree in evangelism. Now that her educational goals had been completed, she began to seek the Lord for a companion again. She wanted children and that old clock was ticking. Gina was at home preparing to go out and feed the homeless when the doorbell rang. It was Sheila.

"Girl, Prophet Joel is coming to town again!"

"No, not Prophet Joel. When?"

"This Friday night. Do you want to go?"

"Do I want to go? Of course, I want to go. I wouldn't miss it. Do you remember years ago when he came and how God spoke through him and told me that I would go to school to receive my degree in engineering and that I would preach the Word? Girl, I didn't even have an interest in engineering and I sure didn't think I'd be preaching. Oh, yes. I'm going! I have been seeking God for a husband and I need a word from the Lord."

Girl, you're not the only one who needs a husband. We are both in the same boat. I will call you Friday around 6 to let you know what time I'm leaving for church so we can go together."

They leave Gina's place and head to the park to feed the homeless.

"You know, Sheila, we need more people who are willing to help the poor. The harvest is truly plentiful but where are the laborers?"

After serving food and ministering they pack up the car. Sheila suggested they go to the mall for a good sale but Gina declined.

"No, I can't go today. I have an appointment. Give me a rain check."

Gina returned home and fell to her knees in prayer.

"God I need you. I am here for our appointment. I am so lonely. I love my girl, Sheila, but I need a husband. My hormones are crazy. I have strong desires to be with a man and it's hard to hold out. I don't want to fall into sin. Please send me a husband. Where is he, God?" Gina continued to weep and question. "God I am 25 years old and I have never been with a man. I have kept myself pure but this is hard. I'm out there feeding the homeless and feeling lonely. I'm out there preaching and I come home alone to an empty house. Is it not your will for me to be married?"

Then in a small still voice, God spoke to Gina's spirit.

"I am with you, Gina. I have heard your request and I know your needs. Be patient and don't hurry. Your season will come."

"Oh Jesus! My season? My season? How long is this season, Lord? A day with you is as a thousand years. I don't have very many childbearing years left Lord. I am 25 years old and I want a family. I want seed in the earth that came from me. How much longer, Lord? How much longer?" Gina cried herself to sleep.

Chapter 3

The Prophecy

"Gina, are you alright?"

"Yes, I'm fine. I just feel in my spirit that God is going to move in this service tonight, Sheila. I came to bless and magnify His name because He is so worthy of my praise. Let's hurry in. I do not want to miss the praise and worship."

They entered the church. The usher offered to escort Evangelist Gina to the pulpit but she declined.

"No thank you. I appreciate your kindness. I will sit here. This seat is just fine."

"What? You didn't want to sit on the pulpit, Gina."

"No, Sheila, not tonight. I'm not sure what God has in store for me but He wants me to sit here and I have learned a long time ago it's just best to obey."

Worshipers were gathered in the sanctuary singing in unity and Gina and Sheila joined in. They lifted their hands high and looked to the ceiling singing *Nobody else like you Jesus; nobody else like you. I could search all over and find nobody else like you. Nobody loves like you Jesus, nobody loves like you. I could search all over and find nobody loves like you."* They basked and praised in God's presence. Some were weeping, some were smiling and dancing. Others bowed down in worship. Gina smiled and in her heart promised to love God with or without a husband

"I still love you, Lord. I am so sorry that I ever doubted you. I believe you will provide for my needs," she cried out to God.

After the sermon, Prophet Joel made an altar call and offered water baptism to those who wanted to be saved.

"We have water here. What hinders you to be baptized in the only name given among us whereby men might be saved? The name of Jesus. What is in your way? Remove all hindrances. You must be born again," he proclaimed.

Many people, old and young, crowded the altar. Some were being filled with the Holy Ghost as they came. As the spirit of God moved in the service, Prophet Joel began to operate in the prophetic gift.

"There is a young woman here who is a preacher. You have been seeking God for a mate. Now don't all you single women preachers come forward. But God has just given me her name. Her name is Gina."

Gina looked at Sheila in amazement and begged Sheila to walk to the front of the church with her.

"Come with me so you can help me remember everything."

"Girl, I am not going up there. Do you see all these people? We might even be on T.V. This is your prophecy, not mine. You'd better buy the tape!"

Gina shook her head at Sheila and walked to the front of the church.

"God I expected a word but not in front of all these people," she thought to herself. "Please don't let him embarrass me.

"It is not him but I that shall speak," the Lord said to Gina in a small still voice

"Are you Gina," the prophet asked.

"Yes, I am.

He laid his hands gently on her forehead and began to pray. After the prayer, he spoke to her what God told him to tell Gina.

"Woman of God, you are about to be given an opportunity to choose between life and death. I admonish you to choose life. You have been praying for a husband and God has heard your prayer. He has asked you to be patient and not hurry. He also says that your season will come. Am I right?"

"Yes you are right," Gina confirmed.

"God has prepared you for a great ministry with your husband-to-be. Your ministry, as well as his, will not only be here in the United States but I see you in Africa preaching the gospel. God says your husband will be revealed in a very short season. Don't be distracted by the enemy. You will reap if you faint not. If you make the wrong choice, you will have a season of much suffering. But God's grace is sufficient. Hear the word of the Lord. You will be tested but be faithful. How can two walk together except they agree? Hold on my sister. God has heard your prayers. Now praise Him!"

Gina spent about 15 minutes on her knees in praise and worship. The prophet continued to call other people to the front for prayer, salvation, and healing. Gina thanked God for the words from heaven and asked Him for direction.

"God, I choose life. I choose life. God, I choose you. I love you, Jesus. I love you."

Chapter 4
Gina Meets Greg

The following week, Gina was at work finishing up a project.

"Whew. I'm hungry. It's time to eat," Gina thought to herself.

"Alright it's lunch time," Gina announced. "Who is the chosen one for the food run today?"

"Not me."

"Not me either. I went the last time."

"I went yesterday."

"I always go," said voices from co-workers.

"Well, I will go today but I am only making one stop and that is to the deli down the street. So write down what you want because I am leaving at 11:30."

"Aw, Gina. We don't want cold food today. We want some fried chicken and collard greens or something."

"Well, Reginald, I guess you'd better go get it yourself, "Mr. Fried Chicken," because I am only going to the deli today."

Laughter filled the office as co-workers chimed in.

"Some folks just have to have grease or they don't feel like they have eaten."

"Yeah, that's why he's so fat now!"

"Alright, alright. That's enough. Hey, last call for orders. I am on my way to the deli. I will have to bring bottled drinks because I can't carry fountain drinks and the food too."

"Come on, Gina, are you sure about the chicken?"

"Yes, Reginald, I'm sure. No chicken for you today my brother."

Gina walked to the deli and noticed a sign that read *Under New Management*. As she walked inside, she smelled the aroma of homemade soups and bread.

"Um it smells good in here," she said savoring the aroma.

"Welcome to Greg's Deli. How may I help you?"

"Hi, thanks. I have a large order for coworkers and myself."

"Sure, I will be glad to help you."

Gina handed over the list of orders to the clerk and strolled around the store. She noticed a tall, handsome man talking to one of the employees. He was the store owner directing employees on how to stock the shelves. Gina thought he was nice looking and well dressed. She was impressed. Gina quickly turned her head when the man noticed her. As she walked over to the counter to pick up the orders, he walked over to her and smiled.

"Such a large order for such a petite woman."

Gina blushed, "This is for my friends at the office. I could never eat all of this."

"Well, I certainly hope you all enjoy it. By the way, my name is Greg. Greg Gaston. I am the new owner. I'd like to offer you 50% off of your next purchase."

"My, how generous of you. That will be great. Is there a coupon or something stating that fact?"

Greg picked up a pen and wrote a note: *Gregory Gaston approves 50% off of...* "What's your name," he asked?

"Gina Mitchell."

"Okay... *of Gina Mitchell's order*. By the way, this expires in five days."

"Five days," Gina replied.

"Oh yes. Five days is about as much time that I can stand between now and the next time I see you."

Gina blushed again, "Thank you," and left the deli. When she returned to the office, she could hardly wait to tell Sheila what happened at the deli.

"Girl, I met the manager of the new deli. His name is Greg Gaston and he gave me 50% off of my next order. He was very handsome too, girl."

"So when are you going back? Tomorrow?"

"No, girl. I wouldn't dare go back the next day. Hmm, let's see, today is Monday. I'll go back on Friday since he gave me five days to use the discount. I don't want to seem desperate, you know."

"Oh but you are," Sheila said as the friends shared a laugh.

"Girl you are a mess. But on a serious note, Sheila, what if he is not saved or living holy?"

"God will save him. Don't you even worry about that," Sheila reassured.

Friday morning Gina took a little longer getting dressed for work.

"This dress is too dark. I need something a little more colorful. Yes, this is it; nice, soft colors with these shoes to match," Gina said, admiring herself in the mirror. "I wonder if he is my husband. God, I asked you to let him come to me and he did. I sure hope this is a sign."

At lunch time Gina gathered the orders and headed to the deli and hoped and prayed he would be there. When she entered the front door, she immediately saw Greg and her heart was relieved. Their eyes met and embraced one another.

"Good afternoon."

"Well, good afternoon to you, Ms. Gina. I am so glad you came by. I was thinking about you this morning and wondering if you would make it in before your coupon expired."

"Now what lady do you know who would pass up a good sale? Fifty percent off is irresistible."

They laughed. Greg went behind the counter to take care of her order.

"May I have the honor of preparing your order ma'am?"

"Why of course you may," Gina blushed. She looked down, pulled her hair behind her ear, and thought to herself, "I don't believe this!"

Greg washed his hands and prepared the sandwiches. He then walked around the counter and handed the food to her with a proud look.

"Thank you, sir. Now that's service!"

"I hope it meets your expectations. May I get the door for you?"

"Well of course but I haven't paid for the food yet."

"Oh, but you did. The moment you walked in the door and I saw your lovely smile was pay enough. You just don't know how many times I called myself a fool the past few days for letting you leave here without getting your phone number. I said 'Man, what were you thinking letting that woman walk out of your life like that.' So I am thankful for a second chance and I won't mess this up believe me. Can we have dinner tonight?"

"Tonight?"

"Yes, tonight. I know you eat more than deli sandwiches."

"Yeah, you are right. I eat a whole lot more; probably too much more!"

"Well if tonight is not good for you, Gina, how about tomorrow?"

"No, Greg. Tonight is fine."

"Great. I will pick you up at 7. Here, write down the directions to your house," he said as he handed her a pen and paper.

"It's real easy to find. Here you are."

"Thanks, Gina, for coming back. You won't regret it. I promise. See you tonight."

"Okay. Bye Greg.

Gina arrived back at the office. As she put the lunches on the table, in walked Sheila with a curious look on her face.

"Well, let's hear it. What happened?"

"Girl, Greg and I are going out to dinner tonight," she whispered. "Can you believe it?"

"Yes, I can believe it. It's your season, girl; your time to reap. It's due, due, due...season! Long overdue," they laughed. "Well, I have to get to know him first. But you never know. He might be the one."

Later that evening at Gina's home, the doorbell rang at 6:50 p.m.

"Oh, my! He's early. I'll be right there."

Gina opened the door and there stood Greg in a black suit, white shirt, and matching tie and handkerchief. His shoes were so shiny you could almost see your reflection. The first thing Gina noticed was his smile and then the bottle of wine in his hand.

"May I come in?"

"Of course. Please do."

"You look lovely tonight, Gina."

"Thank you. I like your suit. It's sharp."

"Do you mind if we have a glass of wine before we go? Our reservation is at 8.

"Well, actually, Greg, I don't drink."

"Not even wine? This has great health benefits."

"Well I have heard of that before but no, not even red wine. Thanks anyway, Greg, that was so thoughtful.

"No, I am sorry. I should have asked you if you drank alcohol before I bought it. That's my fault. I guess we can spend a little time getting to know each other while we wait."

"Sure. That's fine. Would you like some sweet tea?"

"Yes. Tea will be fine."

As Greg got comfortable on the coach, Gina served him tea on ice and sat in the chair across from him.

"Gina, you know I don't bite. You can sit next to me."

"Anything with teeth can bite," she said smiling as she walked over to the couch and sat next to Greg.

"I assure you, Gina, the only thing I am going to bite tonight is a T-bone steak. I am very hungry. So, tell me, how long have you lived here?"

"All of my life. This is home for me. My parents and three siblings still live here also."

"Wow, that's great to have your family in the same city. My family and I haven't lived in the same city for years. My parents are divorced and they both live in New York. I have a sister in Atlanta and a brother in Tennessee. We see one another a few times a year during the holidays or special occasions but we all stay in touch through e-mail, Facebook, Twitter, and by phone, of course. Unfortunately, I am divorced also. My ex-wife and I are still good friends, though. We just got married too young and things didn't work out. Two years after our divorce she got sick and had to be admitted to a nursing home in Columbus Georgia, about a couple hours away."

"I am sorry to hear that. Did you have children?"

"No. No children. I always wanted children, though; at least two or three. How about you, Gina? Do you want children?

"Yes, I want a girl and a boy if it is the Lord's will."

"I bet you can't wait to comb your little girl's hair, huh?"

.   "Oh yes. And put in all those pretty little bows. Children are a blessing. So Greg, do you travel a lot?"

"I used to travel a lot with my different businesses and it was really stressful and hard on my body. I now have regional managers and this has scaled down my frequent flyer miles. Greg's Deli is my baby. I've always wanted a deli with wholesome meats, fruits, and breads. I started the chain five years ago and now have 10 stores nationwide."

"Wow, that's great! You must be proud of your accomplishments."

"Yes, I am but my accomplishments are the result of team effort by many key people who worked very hard. There were times that I went without leisure time, family time, and any other time of enjoyment just to build my business. I even got divorced building a business. But that's in the past. If I had known what I know now I would have done some things differently. I am pretty straight financially and I am ready to settle down, get married, and start a family," he said anxiously awaiting Gina's reply.

"Well, there are certainly plenty of women available. I believe the last count was 12 to 13 women per man in the U.S.

Greg thought to himself, "Wrong answer!" Gina thought to herself, "I know you didn't think I was going to fall for that old marriage line. I don't think so! I'm not that desperate." Greg was concerned that Gina did not acknowledge that she was single and available. Gina did not appreciate being offered wine on the first date. Although their first evening together began and ended on a bad note, they still planned another date. Greg, hoping to create a casual, relaxed environment on the second date, packed a lunch and took Gina on a Saturday picnic to a park about 20 miles from the city.

"This is nice, Greg. Thanks for choosing this area."

"You're welcome. We can just enjoy the scenery without you having to worry about high heels and without me having to worry about a shirt and tie. Let's just lie here on the blanket and enjoy each another.

"Oh boy. I wonder what he means by that? There is only so much we can enjoy of one another," she thought as she took a seat on the blanket.

"You know, I really do owe you an apology for bringing wine to your home on our first date. I guarantee I don't have any today. Are there any particular reasons why you don't drink?"

"Well, I never have except for communion."

"Communion? Are you a frequent church goer?"

"I am a born-again Christian, and a preacher also."

"What! A preacher? Oh no. I offered wine to a preacher? Oh my God! I don't believe it! How long have you been preaching?"

"Just a few years but I have been saved since I was 10."

"Gina that is good. I bet if I had given my life to God when I was young a lot of things would have been different. But I was young and hard headed. I stayed away from church unless I had to go. Maybe I can go with you sometimes?"

"Okay. How about tomorrow," she challenged.

"Tomorrow," said Greg with raised eyebrows. "You sure are quick with the witnessing. I know Jesus now. I may not know Him like you know Him or go to church and all that but I know the Lord," he said in a persuasive tone. If it hadn't been for the Lord I wouldn't be the man I am today or have the things that I have."

28

"Greg, I didn't say you didn't know Jesus. I just asked you to go to church with me."

Okay. I will go. What time should I pick you up?"

"Sunday school starts at 10. I am a teacher so I usually leave home around 9:15. The church is only 10 minutes from my house."

"Woman I must really like you to get up that early on a Sunday. Okay, I will pick you up at 9:15."

Chapter 5
Qualifications for Marriage

Four months later, Gina and Greg were spending more time together.

"Sheila, I did not know I would spend so much time with a man who is not saved. It's time for him to get saved or keep it moving."

"So, what are you gonna do, Gina?"

"I am going to ask him if he loves the Lord and if he wants to give his life to Christ. At this point, he has two of my three criteria for intimacy. It's called the NTM Requirement. If a man wants to get intimate with me, he must give me his name, his time, and his money. Show me the NTM and we can talk. The way I see it, Sheila, if a man loves you, he will want you to have his name, he will spend time with you, and he will spend his money on you. If all women practiced the NTM, we would have less heartache and certainly less sexually transmitted diseases in the world."

"Girl, I know that's right. Most women think just because a man wants sex that he loves them. They need to think again. A dog can have sex if the hormones are working."

They laugh and give each other a high five.

"Seriously, Sheila, even if he has the final N to the NTM, I can't marry him unless we are equal spiritually. Will you pray with me?"

"Sure I will."

Gina believed in the power of prayer. She also asked her pastor to pray with her for God's will to be done concerning her relationship with Greg. But her pastor counseled and instructed her not to get serious with Greg and to remain faithful to prayer and fasting. Gina did pray but her time with God was limited because she spent most of her free time with Greg. He started calling her on church nights and inviting her to go to dinner or to a movie. Gina never missed church before but now she was giving in to Greg and accepting those invitations.

"Gina, you sure are staying out of church a lot these days."

"Sheila, I am dating a real man. I can't be in church all the time. I am there on Sundays and I have only missed mid-week service a few times in the last couple of months."

It's been more than a few, Gina. I can't believe you missed the women's retreat. That was always your favorite event. Don't you think it was strange for Greg to tell you he had tickets to the playoffs and he chose the same day of the retreat?"

"No, I don't think he did it on purpose."

"Well, I do. He does that all the time. He always finds something for you to do on church nights or when you have other plans. Just watch the next time."

"Oh girl, you are so suspicious. I am trying to win a man to Christ. Will you please let me fish!"

"Fish on, my sister! I hope you like what you catch."

On the way to church Sunday morning, Gina asked Greg had he ever seriously thought about giving his life to Christ.

"What I mean is getting baptized in Jesus' name and filled with the Holy Ghost, with the evidence of speaking in tongues?"

"I was just thinking about that this week. I've never been baptized and I do need God's spirit. And, like you said, in order to have God's daughter, I need to be His son. Right? I definitely want His daughter," he said stroking Gina's hair.

Later that day Greg was baptized in Jesus' name. He prayed at the altar for a little while asking God to fill him with the Holy Ghost. He told Gina that he received the Holy Ghost.

"I don't really have to speak in those tongues right away, Gina. A baby doesn't come into the world talking. Give me a little while and I will speak in tongues. I know it is the evidence. I read it in the Bible. They spoke with tongues in Acts 2:1-4. That alter worker lady in the church, Mother Mills, must have read that to me a hundred times," he said shaking his head.

Mother Mills talked to Gina before she left the church with Greg.

"Daughter, now I know you love this man 'cause I can see it in your eyes but he is wrestling with evil. Pure evil I tell you and whatever it is won't let him go until he truly repents. Now I know he was baptized and all but based on what the spirit showed me, honey, he just took a dip in the water. God ain't gonna come in unless you repent and turn away from your sin. Now you know that."

"Yes ma'am, I know but I will keep working with him."

"Honey, it's gonna take God to free him. You be careful! Let the brothers' work with him until he comes through. You don't need to be alone with him anyway."

Across the room, Greg looked at Mother Mills with anger in his eyes as he wondered what she was saying to Gina. Gina grabbed Mother Mills by the hand and softly reassured her that she felt very comfortable around Greg and that she would be alright. She just didn't want to hear any more of Mother Mills' spiritual insight. Gina just knew she had the situation under control. Six months later, God spoke to Gina while she was in prayer.

"Gina, the answer to your prayers is at the door, my child. Continue to wait on me. I have the best for you."

"Yes Lord, I will wait. I will wait."

The phone rang. It was Gina's pastor.

"Gina, this is Pastor Johnson. How are you?"

"I am fine, Pastor. How are you and the family?"

"We are fine. Thanks for asking. Gina, the Lord put on my heart to have a one-night revival next week. Bishop Smith has consented to be our guest speaker. He lost his wife some years ago and, despite many obstacles, his ministry has spread worldwide, even to Africa. Gina, I know this is short notice but I would like for you to lead praise and worship during the service and to also organize a group of the sisters to provide a few light refreshments after the service and serve the clergy."

"Yes Pastor, I can help with that. Consider it done. Give me a call if you think of anything else I can help with."

"Thanks, daughter. I knew I could depend on you. Bless you, now."

On the day of the revival, Greg called Gina.

"Hey, Gina, I have to go away on business in the morning for a couple weeks. Before I leave, there is something very important I have to ask you. You know how much I love you and I believe you love me too. I just don't want to go away for two weeks without being honest with you about how I see our future. I want us to be together, Gina. Can we have dinner tonight?"

"Well Greg, I love you too but I have plans tonight. I am not sure I can meet you."

"Oh, baby come on. Can't you postpone your plans for one night?"

"Well, actually I can't. We are having a revival tonight. Remember? I told you about it last week. The pastor invited a guest speaker from out of town and I have an assignment."

"As big as that church is, I know there is someone else who can take your assignment."

"Well, alright, let me see what I can do and I will call you back."

"Alright, Gina. I'll talk to you later."

Gina hung up the phone from Greg and immediately called Sheila.

"Sheila, girl, I need your help."

"What is it, Gina?"

"I need you to lead praise and worship tonight and to make sure everybody is served refreshments after church, especially the pastor and the guests."

"I thought you were in charge."

"I, I am but Greg has something important to ask me before he leaves town in the morning. He wants to meet for dinner so I am asking you to be in charge in my place."

"Aw girl, here we go again; Greg and his last minute plans. He's pulling you away from church, Gina. I know you are hoping he will ask you to marry him but he can do that after church. Something in my spirit tells me something is just not right about this guy. He is too controlling. He constantly calls you to see where you are and he hardly ever lets you spend time with family and friends. If he does ask you to marry him, you'd better think twice."

"But Sheila I love him. This is what I have been praying for; for my husband to come. I have been waiting a long time for a companion. Nobody is perfect. I know he loves me. He just wants to check on me and make sure I am okay. That's why he calls me so much."

"Yeah, well, it could be something hidden going on like possessiveness or jealousy, or something. I can't put my finger on it, Gina, but I know in my heart that something is not right."

"Well, if you love someone you will be jealous. God is jealous, Sheila. Despite all your accusations, I must say that Greg has been patient with me. He hasn't pushed me to have sex or anything, even though I know it is hard because he is a man. It has been almost a year now and I think we need to move to the next level or stop seeing each other."

"So I guess that means if he asks you to marry him, Gina, you will say yes."

"Yes, Sheila. I will marry him. I want to marry him."

"Well, I hope you are doing the right thing, Gina. Anyway, you need to call Pastor and let him know you won't be at church tonight."

"I will. I am sure he will understand. I am a faithful member. I have always been one of the first to arrive and one of the last to leave. I am sure he will excuse me. Church can go on without me you know."

"I am not saying it can't, Gina, I am just saying you need to see if it's okay for me to help out but if God ordained for you to be there, Gina, you don't want to miss your blessing."

"Look, Sheila, you and I both know how long I have prayed and waited for God to bless me. The blessing is staring me in the face and I believe this is God's will."

"Okay, Gina, just call me back if Pastor okays it. I will be there to help out in any way I can."

Gina called Pastor Johnson and he hesitantly agreed for her to miss the revival.

"Well, Gina, I really sense in my spirit that this revival is a pinnacle for the saints. I envisioned you and others receiving miracles and answers to prayers through this service but if you can't be there, I understand. I pray that whatever God had for you at the revival will remain yours and that you will receive it through the Holy Ghost in due time."

"Thank you, Pastor. I believe and I touch and agree with you that God will bless the service and me even in my absence. We will talk soon."

Gina called Greg but as the phone began to ring, Gina heard a small, quiet voice urging her to go to church tonight.

"Hi Greg, it's Gina."

"Hey, baby. I hope you have good news for me."

Gina rubbed her forehead and prayed silently asking God to forgive her for not going to church and promising to make it up to Him.

"Yes, Greg, I do have good news. I can go to dinner with you tonight."

"Great! I will see you at six sharp."

"Okay, six sharp."

Gina sighed and looked up to the ceiling.

"Lord, was that you telling me to go to church? Lord, why do you want me to go tonight? When I was in college and I had to study for exams, you told me to study some nights. When my mom was sick, you told me to stay home and help her. Now, the man I love might ask me to marry him tonight and you want me to go to church? Please Lord, speak to me and tell me why? Why tonight? Please Lord, speak to me. Don't be quiet now."

The Lord said softly, "Your obedience is better than your sacrifice. Trust me and go to church."

Gina continued to question God as if the answer wasn't good enough. She needed a reason. She even began to reason with God and try to make deals with Him.

"I need to know why, God? Just tell me. Why tonight? I do not want to be disobedient. Okay, Okay, I will go to church after dinner tonight. I will be late but I will get there in time for the Word."

Gina ran upstairs to get dressed for the evening.

Chapter 6
Now Or Never

"Greg, a candle-lit table for two in a five-star restaurant is a lot more than I expected."

"Well, where did you expect me to take the woman I love on this special occasion?

Greg took her hand into his.

"You know, Gina, for the past 11 months you and I have been like white on rice or two peas in a pod. I have gotten used to having you as a part of my day every day. Whenever I'm in a hectic meeting and I see a text message from you, that puts a smile on my face. Gina, you are important to me. Now I know I am not this super spiritual guy who prays all the time but I love God, Gina, and I love you. When I realized I was going to have to travel to take care of one of my businesses, it hit me. I began to think about being away from you for two weeks and I was sad and lonely just thinking about it. I said to myself, I wish Gina could go with me. But knowing you and how you always stress the importance of avoiding the appearance of evil, I know you would never travel with me. So, knowing you will not travel with me as friends, I want to know if you will go with me as my wife. Gina, will you marry me?"

Gina gazed into his eyes.

Meanwhile, at the church, Bishop Smith was preaching a message titled "It's Reaping Time." The powerful message stirred the saints and increased their faith. But on a personal note, Bishop Smith was actually encouraging himself. After losing his wife to breast cancer, he now hoped for a companion with whom he could share his life. Believing God, he trusted that his wife-to-be would be at the service tonight. The Word of the Lord was very clear: *Your wife has been asked to come to church tonight. You will see her tonight if she is obedient. She has been asked to serve you.* Bishop Smith began to wonder whether the mystery woman God had chosen for him knew of God's plans for the would-be couple.

As he looked out into the congregation of hundreds, a great anointing fell upon him and he asked, "Is there anyone in the house tonight who is ready to receive?"

The congregation shouted in loud voices declaring they were ready to receive, ready to reap the blessings of God. The church erupted in praises and dancing filled the sanctuary.

"Some of you have been waiting for 10 years or more. It doesn't matter how long you have been waiting. The question is will you receive from the Lord. For some of you, it's healing in your body; for others, it's healing in your spirit. Some of you may be waiting on a financial breakthrough. And some of you need to accept the best blessing of all - God's salvation. What a great salvation. Whatever it is that you need, Jesus is in the room. Receive, receive! Tell the Lord any way you bless me, Lord, I will be satisfied."

Bishop Smith continued to minister and many people were rejoicing. Some were getting out of their wheelchairs. Wealthy people were bringing money to the altar to give to the less fortunate and teenagers began rededicating their lives to the Lord. After the alter call and benediction, Bishop Smith went to the pastor's study to freshen up and change clothes. He could hardly wait to go to the dining hall for refreshments. He had great expectations.

"Lord, I sure hope she is here."

He reminisced on the vision God had given him of the beautiful woman who was to be his wife. She had long, brown hair and a perfect smile. She was ministering and singing praises to God with a powerful anointing. He could never forget her face. The image of her beauty remained in his heart. Before walking out of the study, he kneeled down to pray. It was a prayer of thanksgiving for his bride. The years after his wife's death were spent grieving and healing. He committed to waiting three years to equal the three years God had given them together. And now, he was ready to find a wife and start a new life with her. After all the praying and fasting, he expected to see her tonight. He opened the door and walked toward the dining hall.

Back at the restaurant, Greg kissed Gina's hand and reached into his coat pocket for the small, burgundy ring box. The three-karat diamond ring sparkled.

"This is beautiful, Greg. I love you, too.Yes.Yes. I will marry you."

 Greg put the ring on her finger.

"Gina, let's eat so you can go home and pack."

Startled, Gina said, "Pack! You really want me to go with you now?"

"Yes, let's just elope. We can get married while we are in New York. I promise I won't touch you until we are married."

"It's not that, Greg. You have been more than a gentleman toward me but it's just that I want a wedding and I have not met your family yet. I've only talked to them on the phone."

"You can meet my parents while we are in New York. Listen, Gina, I had a wedding with my first wife and, to tell you the truth, we should have invested that money. We spent thousands of dollars for one event that was over in two to three hours. People came and ate up all the food, talked negatively about the wedding colors, who was in the wedding, and anything else they could think of, and most of them didn't even bring a gift. A wedding is just not a good investment, Gina."

"Well, I understand how you feel, Greg. What if we just keep it small; just family and a few friends?"

"Well, okay, Gina, just as long as I can have you when it's all over."

"Yes, you can, most gladly."

Gina looked at her watch. Oh no. It's 8:30 and I still need to go by the church."

"Church? I thought you were going to spend this evening with me!"

"Well I am but I made a promise that I have to keep."

"Okay. So I guess that is more important than being with your fiancé on the last evening he is in town. You can go to church two weeks straight starting in the morning if you want to but I really want you to be with me tonight, Gina. Don't leave me, baby."

In her heart, Gina prayed. She questioned why this was such a hard decision and why she was so confused. Just then, she heard a loud voice say, "You'd better stay here with this man. You can go to church anytime."

Greg smiled, "Well, Gina, are you leaving me or what?"

"No Greg. I am not leaving you. Can you stop me by the church on the way home so I can be sure everything is straight?"

"Sure baby. I can do that."

They continued to talk about their future together.

"I want to buy a house for you - one you can decorate yourself, choose your own colors and furniture. Would you like that, Gina?"

"Yes, Greg. Can I have help from a decorator?"

"Sure baby, sure. Anything you want."

42

The longer Greg talked the more Gina looked at her watch. Even though she was happy to be engaged to Greg, for some reason she felt an urgency to go to church.

"Greg, I really think we need to go now."

"Okay honey. Let's run by the church if it will make you happy."

They arrived at the church at 10:15. Pastor Johnson was walking Bishop Smith to the front door. You were rather quiet at the reception, my friend, and it is unusual for you to stay until the last guest leaves. You really did not have to do that you know."

"Yes, I know. Pastor, are you sure that all of the servers were here tonight that was supposed to come?"

"I believe they were. It was arranged by one of the sisters so I am not sure. Why do you ask?"

Bishop Smith began to tell Pastor Johnson about his vision. The conversation was interrupted when Pastor Johnson's cell phone rang.

"I'm sorry. Excuse me a moment, Bishop."

He took the call and then returned to the conversation.

"Now, what were you saying, Bishop?"

Just then Bishop Smith's driver pulled the car around to the curb and blew the horn.

"Oh never mind. That's okay. Thanks again for the invitation, Pastor. I will be in touch."

He shook hands with the pastor, walked out the door, and got into the car. As the car drove away, Bishop Smith disappointedly looked out of the window at the city lights and skyscrapers. A few moments later, Gina and Greg walked in from the rear of the church. Most of the lights were off and Pastor Johnson and one of the deacons were locking the doors.

"Praise the Lord, Pastor. How was service?"

"Praise the Lord, Gina. Hello, Greg. Church service was phenomenal. The Lord really blessed tonight. As a matter of fact, you just missed the guest speaker. Deacon Hall took him to the hotel not even five minutes ago. We were here fellowshipping for a little while after service. He brought the Word forth and many souls were saved and blessed."

"Pastor, that's great! I do hate we missed it."

"Well, Gina, we have it on CD and DVD. If you would like one, just go by the media center when you get a chance."

"Okay. I know it's late, Pastor, but Greg and I want you to be the first to know that we are engaged to be married. He proposed to me tonight."

Pastor Johnson hesitated a moment then said dryly, "Well, we bless God for the both of you. I am always here if you need me. Have a good night." He waved and walked toward his car.

"Gina, for some reason I did not get good vibes from your pastor."

"Greg, he is more like a father to me. I have been in this church since I was a baby. He probably thought you should have asked him for my hand in marriage."

"I did not even ask your real father so why would I ask him? I am not old fashioned. Is that important to you, that I ask your father?"

"No, please don't. Let me talk to him first."

Chapter 7
It's Official

The room was quiet when Gina announced the engagement to her parents.

"Are you sure honey? I mean you haven't known him very long. And you know he never did receive the Holy Ghost."

"Mom, he asked God to save him and fill him and we believe that the evidence will come. I love him. He is a good man and I believe he really loves the Lord."

With his glasses pushed down off his nose Gina's father said in his deep, baritone voice, "Yeah, but what about being unequally yoked? The Word is the Word and how can two walk together except they agree?"

"Oh, but we do agree, Daddy. I sometimes wonder if we take that scripture out of context. He is not an idol worshiper or occultist. He goes to church and believes Jesus came in the flesh as I do. Now please, Mom, please Dad, don't drill me with sermons about salvation. Only God knows who belongs to Him and who belongs to the devil. I believe Greg is of God and I want to be his wife."

Gina's mother allowed anger to take over as she threw the dishtowel on the table.

"Girl, you are blinded right about now. You couldn't see who he really is if it shined bright in your face. Well, I am not in love with him and neither is your father. You'd better listen to people whose eyes are opened and can see that this is not your husband!"

"Enough Mama! I don't want to discuss this anymore. What do you want me to do, marry someone like daddy, a preacher? Everybody is not a preacher or teacher or even strong in the Lord. Yes, Greg may be a babe in Christ or even a weak saint but he is a part of the body of Christ."

"And just how and when did he become a part of the body of Christ, Gina. I want to know!"

Daddy, please don't do this. He was baptized in Jesus' name just like you, and I believe he will be filled with the Holy Ghost in due time."

"Well, just wait 'till he's filled then, baby. When his due time comes, then the marriage will come. Your father and I want the best for you. And you can believe I have the Word to back me up."

"So does this mean you will not support my marriage?"

"Honey, how can you expect something to stand if the foundation is wrong? Standing by a house that is sinking will do little good. The best bet is to get out of the way so it does not fall on you."

Gina's father could take no more. He rubbed his partially bald head in confusion and walked out of the room. Gina looked at her mother with tears in her eyes.

"You, too, Mom? Are you going to just abandon me, too?"

"No, Gina. I am not going to abandon you and neither will your father. We do not approve of your decision but we still love you and will be praying much for you."

"That's what I need, Mama. I need your prayers." As they embraced, Gina's mother remembered the dream she had nearly a year ago and tears ran down her cheeks.

Later that evening, Gina told Sheila about the engagement.

"Not you, too, Sheila. You are my girl. Even though you have your doubts, I thought you would support me."

"Gina I do support you. It's just that something about Greg is not quite adding up. Why is his ex-wife in a nursing home and she's only in her 30s? What happened to her? Why did they divorce? Why won't he let you meet his family? Why did he want to elope? He has been married before but you are a virgin and have never been married. Why would he try to talk you into eloping? I don't know, Gina, something just isn't right. And let's not forget his controlling behavior. Just wait until you are married. I don't think you will be hanging out with me, that's for sure."

"Well, Sheila, I know we won't be able to hang out like we used to because I will be a wife but we can still go shopping and go on outings and stuff. You're my girl. You know that."

"Well, if I am your girl, do me a favor. Let's go visit his ex-wife and see what she has to say about him."

"Sheila I don't even know what nursing home she is in."

"I am sure we can find out on the internet with all of these find-a-loved-one sites out there."

"Sheila, what are we trying to prove? No matter what she says, there are always two sides to every story, or should I say three sides - his side, her side, and the truth."

"Well, Gina, let's get her side and go from there."

They searched online and located Greg's ex-wife at a nursing home in Columbus. Two weeks later, Gina and Sheila took a trip to see her.

"I can't believe we are here in Columbus getting ready to visit Greg's ex-wife. Sheila, I'm nervous about this."

"Come on, Gina, let's do this."

They walked into the building and told the front desk clerk they wanted to see Ms. Gaston.

"Sign in. I need to see your ID please."

After showing the clerk their drivers' licenses, they were directed to room 218 just down the hall to the left.

"Gina, I wonder how she looks. I wonder if she can talk. 216, 217, well, here we go. This is it, Gina. Let's go."

Gina and Sheila walked into the room. There sat a pretty, thin young woman with long black hair. She was looking at the ceiling and her eyes were somewhat crossed. Her upper lip was slanted to one side and old scars were visible on her face. Her frail body shook as she moved the blanket over her legs.

"Oh my God! Look at her. Gina! I know you'd better rethink this," Sheila whispered. "If being married to him leaves you like this, you'd better leave town now."

"Be quite, Sheila. She might hear you. Ah hem, hello. Ah, my name is Gina. I am a minister. You don't know me but, ah, I just wanted to meet you and, and say hello. How are you?"

The lady shook her head as if to say she was okay but did not speak.

"This is my friend, Sheila. We would love to spend some time with you and encourage your heart."

Ms. Gaston smiled.

"Let's begin by reading a few scriptures then we will pray and sing some songs. Is that okay?"

She nodded her head yes. Sheila could hardly wait for Gina to finish the last scripture.

"Okay. Great service. Uhh, Ms. Gaston, before we leave we want you to share with us some of your memories of your marriage to Mr. Gaston. How was your marriage? Did you have a happy marriage?"

Gina nudged Sheila very hard and said, "Don't do that now. Well, when then?"

Ms. Gaston began moving around in her chair and shaking her head from side to side as if to say no.

"I am so sorry, Ms. Gaston. Sheila and I did not mean to upset you."

"Well, she was fine until we asked her about her marriage, Gina. Strike three! He's out. You see Ms. Gaston, your ex-husband wants to marry my friend, Gina, and we were really hoping you could shed some light on how he was as a husband."

Ms. Gaston became more irritable and started to cry and pull at her blanket. Tears streamed down her face. The nurse came in and told Gina and Sheila they had to leave.

"It looks like she has gotten upset about something. It is very important that she remains calm. You must leave at once."

"Okay. We will leave," Gina said as she rolled her eyes at Sheila.

"What? I did not do anything but mention her ex-husband's name, Gina. It's the memory of him that upset her, not me!"

"Let's just go, Sheila."

"Okay, Gina. But listen. Even though Ms. Gaston did not say anything, if she could, I believe she would have told you to run for your life!"

"Sheila, that woman is sick and confused. She probably does that all the time when challenged with questions."

"Gina, why are you so blind? Where is your brain? Have you lost your mind or something? That lady was scared. I saw it in her eyes."

"No, Sheila. What you saw was a lady who was being visited by total strangers and became a little uneasy."

"Girl, do you know how many strangers visit nursing homes every day? Many people and animals, too, for that matter, come to nursing homes to visit. That lady was fine until I asked her about her marriage. Please, Gina don't be so stupid."

"I am not being stupid, Sheila. If the shoe fits for stupidity, then you wear it 'cause I am not."

Gina was very angry.

"Are you going to mention this visit to Greg?"

"Why should I, Sheila?"

"Why should you? Ask him what happened to his ex-wife who looks to be in her late 30s, early 40s'. Ask him if she had a stroke or what?"

"Sheila, now you know that is personal information he will not disclose."

"I bet he would if he wanted to marry me. I would insist! He is just too secretive and he isolates you, Gina. He keeps tabs on you minute by minute. I mean you might as well wear a prison monitor and remain under house arrest. Not to mention the fact that the closest he has gotten to receiving the Holy Ghost is reading an old Casper the Friendly Ghost comic book."

"Sheila, how do you know what he has? Are you God?"

"No, I am not and neither are you. So you had better get to asking God who knows the heart of every man."

"Gina let anger get the best of her and she began to wonder whether Sheila was just jealous of her because she was getting married before her.

"Well, you can just talk on, Sheila, because I am not going to miss my blessing messing around with you. God sent me a word through Prophet Joel about my husband and my ministry and now it is my time."

"That's my point, Gina. He also said that you would be given the right to choose between life and death."

"Correct! And I choose life. I choose to marry rather than burn in my flesh and perhaps fornicate and then burn in hell. If you are really my friend, then just pray for me."

"I am praying for you, Gina. I am. But you know as well as I do that our prayers have got to line up with the Word of God. If you believe the word that came through Prophet Joel as a man of God, then how are you going to minister in Africa? Greg has already told you that he is not going to Africa."

"Well, he doesn't have to go, Sheila."

"Oh, and do you honestly think he will let you go all the way to Africa by yourself?

"Yes, I know he will. God knows all things, Sheila. Let's just trust Him."

They drove home in complete silence. The only sound in the car was from the CD Gina finally put in to keep her awake while driving.

Chapter 8

Short Lived Happiness

It was a beautiful Saturday afternoon. The sun was shining brightly and the birds were singing. A perfect day for a wedding. Gina was dressed in a beautiful floor-length, white gown with lace and pearl accents. Her shoulder-length hair was covered with an elegant veil. With Sheila by her side, she looked at herself in the mirror and wiped away tears.

"I can't believe I am getting married today."

"It's not too late to change your mind, you know. I can get your mom and dad and tell them you've changed your mind. They can tell Greg."

"No, Sheila. These are tears of joy. I am so happy that in one hour I will be Mrs. Gregory Gaston. God is so good to have blessed me with such a fine man."

"Okay, Gina. I promise you this one thing. No matter what happens, I will always be there for you. I will always be your friend and your prayer partner, no matter what. Just remember that. Okay?"

"I will, Sheila."

"Alright then. This is it. Let's go. Your groom awaits," Sheila said as looked upward and prayed, *Lord, help us.*

The sanctuary was beautifully decorated with red and white roses. White, paper doves hung from the ceiling, representing the Holy Spirit. As Gina walked down the aisle, Greg began to sing a song that he wrote about the joy of marrying a beautiful woman. Gina thought to herself, *"I thought they were supposed to play the bridal march like they did in the rehearsal."* Sheila thought to herself, *"Oh Lord! That Greg is taking over again."* Sheila took her place beside Gina as her maid of honor while Greg continued to sing the song. He hit a high note and kneeled at Gina's feet. The congregation of witnesses went crazy clapping and cheering. Greg completed the song, stood to his feet, and wiped the tears from Gina's eyes with his handkerchief.

Bishop Johnson began the ceremony.

"Who gives this woman to be wed?"

After a moment of silence, Gina's father looked at Greg with the most displeased look anyone could ever have and huffily said, "I do." He quickly took a seat beside his wife. Gina's mom held his hand as he sat there shaking his head.

Bishop Johnson continued.

"We have come today to join together this man and woman in holy matrimony. If there is anyone here that knows any reason why these two should not be married speak now or forever hold your peace."

Sheila thought to herself, *"Would somebody please say something so my friend can know what kind of man this is?"* No one said a word. Gina looked out at Greg's parents as they smiled. Shelia, still thinking to herself, was hoping for a last minute cancellation. She peered at Greg's parents and thought to herself, *I know you two oughta know something. Come on now. Just say it. Say it.*

The ceremony continued, Gina and Greg exchanged vows, the pastor prayed, and the happy couple kissed softly on the lips. Greg then followed with a kiss to Gina's forehead.

"I love you, baby. Thank you for marrying me. This is the greatest day of my life."

"I love you too, Greg."

They embraced tightly as the audience applauded. Gina smiled and held Greg's arm gently as he guided her down the pulpit stairs. The music played softly and they walked out of the sanctuary. Gina's mom could not hold back the tears. She cried loudly as if she was at a funeral instead of a wedding. She couldn't help but remember the dream she had and the vivid picture of Gina in a wedding dress smiling as she walked into a black hole. Mr. Mitchell hugged his wife to console her.

"It's okay. We did all we could. God will have to do the rest. She was God's child before she was ours so don't worry. The Lord won't let her down. No matter what, God promised to be with his children always. She is under the blood and no devil can have her. Do you hear me?" He wipes her tears away and looked into her eyes. "No devil can pluck her out of God's hand." He said.

"I know but it hurts so much to see my child make such a serious mistake."

Greg and Gina laughed and cuddled in the hallway of the church. "We did it, Greg. We are husband and wife."

"Yes, baby, we did. Now let's cut the reception short. We have a plane to catch in the morning and we need some rest."

"Okay, Greg, but we have to take pictures and cut the cake. It shouldn't take long. I don't want to leave before greeting everyone, though."

Gina interrupted the conversation to speak to a guest.

"Praise the Lord, Sis. Emma."

Greg glared at her with a look of disgust on his face. Gina's mom walked over and hugged her.

"You are so beautiful, baby."

"Thank you, Mama. Thank you for your prayers also. Greg wants us to leave early so we can get some rest before we take our flight to Hawaii."

"Early? Gina, this is your wedding reception. How are you going to leave early? Some of these people have driven long distances to see you, Gina. I know you are not just going to disappear. Your plane doesn't leave until 1 o'clock tomorrow."

"No, I won't disappear, Mama. We just can't stay long."

"Gina, he has waited this long for you, surely he can wait a few more hours."

"Mama, please don't start. I will stay to greet the guests. Don't worry."

Three hours later Greg and Gina walked into their hotel room. Greg had been quiet during the entire drive to the hotel.

They walked into the hotel room. "Honey, what's wrong?" Gina said as she put her hand on Greg's shoulder.

"What's wrong? What's wrong?" Greg said. He snatched her hand off of his shoulder and squeezed her hand tightly until she fell to the floor on her knees.

"Why are you playing dumb, Gina? You know what is wrong."

"Greg, please stop. That hurts. Why are you mad?" Her hand began to turn red as he continued to twist her fingers.

"Why am I mad, Gina?"

"I don't know Greg. Please. It hurts!"

"What did I tell you, Gina? I told you that I did not want to be at that church all day. Didn't I?"

He released her hand and walked around in the room shaking his head.

"Yes, Greg, I know what you said."

Gina rubbed her right hand and examined it.

"Greg, the time just flew by and I thought you were enjoying yourself, too."

"Well, you thought wrong. This is my day. I am the one who is supposed to be enjoying you not all your family and friends. You have been putting them before me long enough. Now you are my wife and what I say goes. Do you hear me?"

He grabbed her face and pulled her toward him.

"Yes, Greg, I hear you."

He walked into the bathroom and turned on the shower as he continued to yell at Gina.

"Now it is my wedding night and I am dog tired."

Gina grabbed some tissue and began to cry with her mouth covered so Greg could not hear her yelling. The pain that she felt in her hand could not compare to the pain she felt in her heart. Never had she seen Greg act this way, and, for the first time, she wished she had never met him. She thought to herself, *Lord, I don't believe this. He is crazy.* While Greg was in the shower, Gina fell asleep in a chair with her head resting on the table. Twenty minutes later Greg came out of the bathroom dressed for bed. He walked over to Gina and gently touched her shoulder. Startled, Gina jumped up.

"What!"

"I am sorry, baby. I don't ever want to hurt you. Please forgive me. I am just exhausted and stressed out. I wanted this to be a special night for us and I did not want to be worn out that's all."

Gina was silent. Greg stood her up and embraced her.

"I am truly sorry Gina, truly sorry. Let me see your hand. How does it feel?"

Gina allowed him to see her hand.

"It's alright, Greg."

"I am glad," he said as he kissed her fingers. "I have some bath water ready for you."

Gina grabbed her small suitcase and walked into the bathroom. She kneeled at the tub and began to pray. "Lord, I am scared. I don't like what just happened. It is not right and I do not want to live this way. I feel like I should leave now and never look back but I just married this man today. Lord, please help us. Please, Jesus."

Gina bathed for a long time, dreading what Greg had in store for her when she returned to the bedroom. While looking through her suitcase, she wished she had an Eskimo suit to wear. *I don't want him to see me naked. Oh, look at all this lingerie'. I do not want to wear any of these. I don't want him to touch me now.* Gina had no choice but to wear one of the attractive nightgowns because that was all she packed. Meanwhile, in the bedroom, Greg put the apple cider on ice and turned on some soft music. When Gina came out of the bathroom, Greg admiringly looked at her.

"Gina, I want this night to be special for you," he said as he held her around the waist and walked her toward the glasses of cider. "I promise I will never hurt you again. It happened once but it will not happen again. You mean the world to me and I love you. I consider myself lucky to have you as my wife."

Greg made a toast to Gina. "To the love of my life."

With her bruised hand, Gina lifted the glass to her lips and took a small sip. Greg gently removed her lace robe.

Greg held Gina softly and said, "I have waited so long for this moment, Gina."

For the first time, Gina gave herself to a man sexually. Greg made passionate love to her as if nothing wrong had ever happened. The next day, they flew to Hawaii and continued their two-week honeymoon. While in Hawaii, Greg was a perfect gentleman. He did not hurt or yell at Gina. When they arrived home, Gina ran into an old friend from college at the airport.

"Gina!"

"Kurt!"

They gave each other a friendly embrace.

"Sister, how are you? I hear you got married. I hate I missed the wedding. Congratulations."

"Thank you, Kurt. I am actually just returning from my honeymoon."

Well, that is great, Gina. Carroll and I still plan to wed next year when she finishes grad school."

Kurt took Gina's hand and continued to talk.

"It is so good to see you, Gina. How is your ministry?"

"It is blessed."

"Well, you know you will be hearing from us soon about speaking at our annual leadership conference."

From a distance, Greg became very angry as he watched Gina and Kurt hold a cheerful conversation giggling about the good old college days. Greg walked over to them and smiled.

"Greg, I would like for you to meet Brother Kurt Brown. He and I went to college together."

"Hello, Kurt," he said as he gave Kurt a cordial handshake.

"Good to meet you man and congratulations on your wedding. You married a blessed woman. She is one anointed preacher."

"Yes, she is. Thanks. Gina, are you about ready?"

Greg began to walk toward the exit.

"Sure Greg. Well, Kurt, I look forward to hearing from you. Tell Carroll I said hello."

"Okay, Gina, you take care and call me if you ever need anything."

Greg's anger escalated.

"What does he mean call if you need anything? Is he out of his mind or something? If you need anything, I am your husband and I will get whatever you need. Not him! I think he was coming on to you, Gina, and I don't want you calling him at all, period. Not for a preaching engagement or anything else."

"Greg he's just a friend and besides, he's engaged to be married. I don't care if he is engaged. He is a man who had his arms around my wife and was holding my wife's hand."

"Greg we were just greeting one another."

"Shut up Gina! My wife does not greet another man with a hug and kiss ever. Do you get that?"

He pulled her closer to him, ripping a button from her blouse.

"Okay, okay, Greg. I won't do it again. I promise."

Gina was so embarrassed as she tried to keep down the commotion that was drawing attention to them. That Sunday at church, Gina made sure to give very little attention to the brothers. She waved from a distance or shook their hands quickly. Greg's eyes were on her constantly. A brother eventually approached her.

"Are you singing on the praise team today, Gina? No. Not today. I plan to be back next week. I have been gone for two weeks and I need to practice."

"Alright, I can't wait to hear your voice. You were really missed."

"Pray for me. To God be the Glory."

As she walked away quickly toward Greg, Gina thought to herself, *now I know he is not going to hit me in church*. She nervously sat down next to Greg and grabbed the hymnbook.

"Would you like to share the book, Greg?

"Sure, Gina. You know I like to hear you sing, too. But I don't think you need to be on the praise team now that you are married. You can sing from your seat and at home."

"What do you mean, Greg?"

"We will talk about it when we get home, Gina. Now bring the book a little closer."

Gina moved the hymnbook closer to Greg and reached in her pocket for a tissue to wipe her tears. Two single sisters looked at Greg and Gina and admired the couple.

"Look at Gina and her husband. Isn't that sweet how they are worshiping together," they continued to speculate. "Gina is so happy that tears are rolling down her face. God has truly blessed her."

The other sister agreed.

"Yeah, she has a good looking, rich man. And I heard he told her she doesn't have to work as a chemical engineer anymore. She can stay home and be a housewife. Now ain't that the life?"

"Hmm, I would be a housewife anytime. I wish God would send me a man like him. I would surely take him. I wonder if he has a brother."

They laughed a moment then joined in singing the congregational hymn. Pastor Johnson's message was *Don't Judge a Book by Its Cover*. Though man looks at the outer part, God looks at the heart. Gina wept even harder as she meditated on the sermon. *God, what was I thinking? You knew the type of man I was marrying and I only saw his outward parts.*

"Gina, why are you crying so much," Greg whispered?

"The Word is so powerful that's all."

"Well, I wish you would go to the bathroom and powder your nose or something."

"Okay, Greg, I will be back."

All over the sanctuary, people were standing up, clapping, and rejoicing over the Word of God. On the way to the bathroom, Gina fell to her knees praising God.

"Lord, you are the one that reigns in the heart and I praise you, Lord! Hallelujah, hallelujah, hallelujah. No matter what I go through, Lord, I praise you because you are worthy. The devil can't stop my praise."

She began to dance and shout as the praise music was played at the end of the message.

"Go ahead, Sister Gina," said one of the single sisters as she fanned Gina and encouraged her to continue praising God. "Praise your God. You owe Him praise. You are a blessed woman." The sister then looked over at Greg who turned his head and looked the other way.

After church Greg walked Gina to the car. She was very drunk in the spirit and laughed for joy as she stumbled through the parking lot. "Oh God is so good," she praised.

"Gina, if you are going to be acting like this in church, you will not be coming back anymore. This is downright uncalled for. You have totally embarrassed me. I never liked all that Holy Ghost jumping around anyway."

Gina tried to be quiet but her lips continued to tremor as she spoke quietly in her heavenly language. She leaned her head against the window and didn't say a word to Greg. Greg drove the car recklessly, burning the tire rubber as he turned street corners. Gina grabbed her seatbelt and prayed to herself, asking God to get her home safely.

"Okay, Gina. Enough is enough! These are the rules starting today. No praise team, no choir, no dancing and shouting in church while I am there, and no preaching either. You need to be at home with me. You don't need to be up in some church all the time. Do you hear me?"

"Yes, Greg, I hear you. Lord I bless you in this storm," Gina whispered.

Greg said, "Shut up Gina" as he slapped her. "I mean shut your dog on mouth woman! You wait till I get you home."

Greg pulled the car into the driveway.

"Get out of the car now!"

Gina opened the door and walked toward the house while Greg pulled off in a rage leaving without a word of explanation. Gina went to the bedroom and kneeled down to pray. Again, Gina asked God to protect her and keep her safe.

"God I just don't know what to do. I can't minister in song anymore. He has taken everything from me. I don't even want to think of my life without being able to share the gifts you have given me. Please touch his heart. Don't let this be, Lord. I love you and I want to serve you. Devil, you are a liar. I rebuke you now in the name of Jesus! You loose my husband and let him go!"

Gina ended her prayer and sat down alone to eat dinner. Later that evening when Greg returned home and opened the door, Gina did not know what to expect. Hoping that he had calmed down and was not thinking of hitting her, she looked him in his eyes and asked if he was okay. As if by divine intervention, Greg did not hit her.

"Yes, I am fine."

"Are you hungry?"

"No, I ate earlier. Thanks."

He walked upstairs, took a shower, and got into bed. Gina put away the leftover food and cleaned the kitchen. After reading a book for an hour, she walked upstairs to prepare for bed. *God I hope he is already asleep*, she thought but he was awake. Greg looked at Gina and apologized for his behavior.

"Look, Gina, I am going to get some help tomorrow. I heard that they have anger management classes at the hospital. I will look into it."

"Greg, you need more than anger management. You need to go somewhere to get help for abuse."

"Abuse? Oh so now I am an abuser, huh? Just because I take authority in my house makes me an abuser?" He said as he sat up in the bed. "That does not mean that I am an abuser. A man ain't a man if he doesn't know how to take control of his own woman. If I go to something like that they might ask too many questions. I will go to the anger classes and that is all. Now I've admitted that I have a problem and I am going to get help. Okay?"

Though she said okay, Gina doubted in her heart that he would attend the anger management classes. The following week Greg sat in on a group counseling session with a therapist and four other men who confessed to having anger and abuse episodes against their spouses or significant others.

"You know I don't even believe I have a problem," said one of the attendees. "My wife is the problem; her and her big mouth. She talks too much so I have to shut her up! You see, she has a problem with headship. I am the man and I am the head. What I say goes. I don't need her input. If I need it, I will ask for it."

"And how does it make you feel when your wife gives you advice," asked the therapist.

"It makes me feel like a kid or something. Like I'm stupid or something."

"And what about you, Mr. Gaston? What triggers your anger?"

Greg looked at her and the rest of the group and responded, "You know what? I am sorry. I don't belong here. I am sorry for the inconvenience." He stood up and walked out.

Chapter 9
The Abuse Continues

One year later Gina was in the kitchen preparing dinner. Most of her day was spent cleaning the house, doing laundry, and ironing. She took a plate, nicely prepared and garnished to Greg in the dining room.

"I hope you like it. It's honey braised chicken. Your favorite. I want to go to Bible study tonight if that's okay."

Greg hadn't gone to church in a long time. With his eyes full of anger, Greg put a piece of chicken in his mouth and chewed slowly before giving Gina an answer.

"You should be able to study the Bible at home. Why do you have to go to church; because man says it?"

"No, Greg, actually the Bible says we are to assemble ourselves together."

Greg reached across the table and slapped her with all his strength.

"Now that will be the last scripture you quote to me. You ain't going nowhere. You can clean this nasty house that is what you can do. Now study that!"

Gina held her face and cried in pain. She picked up the piece of chicken from the floor that fell from her mouth and placed it on a napkin.

"Greg, why did you hit me?"

"Because you deserve it. That's why. You make me hit you because of the stupid stuff you say."

Gina looked at him with tears in her eyes.

"You haven't spoken decently to me in months. I feel like I am being raped when we have sex, and you constantly abuse me. How could I deserve this?"

"Look, woman, you are blessed and don't even know it. Plenty of women would love to live in this million-dollar house with me and get all of this, and this." Greg pointed to himself and opened his arms wide as he looked around the elegant home they lived in. "Now start counting your blessings."

He grabbed his plate and walked upstairs. Gina pushed her plate aside and wept bitterly. Just then, the phone rang. Hey, Gina, this is Sheila. Are you going to church tonight?"

As she looked in the mirror at her swollen lip, she answered. "No, Sheila, not tonight. I have a few things I have to do for Greg."

"Sounds like you've been crying, Gina. What do you have to do for him; stay home and nurse the wounds he keeps putting on you so no one else can see them? Gina, how long are you going to take this? This man hurt you on your wedding night. You should have got an annulment then. Now here you are one year later and you're still getting beat. How long is it going to take for you to realize that he was not the one?"

"I have thought about it over and over again. Why did I marry him, why? I don't know how much longer I can take this life, Sheila. I was hoping he would get better. Yes, I made a big mistake by marrying him and I have to suffer I guess."

"No, you don't either. You'd better get up out of there and leave that crazy man."

"It is not that easy to make a choice like that, Sheila."

"Life isn't easy and we do have to make difficult choices sometimes, Gina. The choice is yours whether to leave Greg or stay.

Believe it or not, by staying in this mess you have already made a choice. Are you happy Gina?"

"No"

"When was the last time you enjoyed life? When was the last time you took a walk or had a good laugh?"

"Those are good questions and honestly I can't remember the last time I walked or exercised, but I did have a good laugh in the Holy ghost at church service some months ago. That is until Greg quenched the Spirit."

"Gina, come here," Greg yelled.

"Okay. I'll be right there! Look, Sheila, I have to go. You know I am so glad that you are my friend. Thank you. I have to go but come by tomorrow if you can. Greg will be out of town for a week. He is leaving in the morning, thank God."

"Okay, Gina, I'll see you tomorrow after work."

Gina hung up the phone and slowly walked upstairs.

"Yes, Greg."

"Come here."

He held Gina in his arms.

"I'm sorry, baby, for hitting you. I had a stressful day and I was wrong. Please forgive me. I am going to get some help I promise. Do you forgive me?"

"Of course I do."

He kissed her gently and said, "I love you woman. I need you in my life. Promise me you won't leave me."

Greg, I don't want to leave you. Please get some help as soon as you get back in town."

Okay, I will. You can choose the therapist, Gina, but I'll make the appointment. Okay?"

"Okay, Greg, it's a deal."

The next evening Sheila came over as promised.

"Hey, Gina, How was your day?"

"It was okay. I just rested and did a little laundry."

"Do you think Greg will ever let you go back to work?"

No. He says I don't need to work. Keeping the house is my job now and of course, he wants children next year."

"Well, what do you want?"

"I want a family. I just want a nice, happy family but I don't want to bring children into an abusive home either."

"So what happened after he busted your lip this time?"

"The usual. He begged my forgiveness, promised to get help, and made passionate love to me. He never gets the help he so desperately needs. He always makes excuses for leaving the group."

"Passionate lovemaking?" Well, it's too bad that couldn't happen without the busted lips and black eyes he's been giving you. I wouldn't wait for him to get help. Let him get help on his own. You have heard his lies long enough. Gina, I am afraid that this lunatic is going to kill you and I will spend the rest of my life feeling guilty for not turning him in. You have to protect yourself. I have something for you," she said as she pulled a small box from her gym bag. "Have you ever heard the saying that a woman has to do what a woman has to do? Well, I bought you a gun just in case you have to do what you have to do. You never know, Gina. One day it may come down to you or him and I want you to be able to make the right choice. This fool is crazy and you know he is crazy and he will kill you and get off on an insanity plea. Now, first of all, you need to report him to the police and get a restraining order. Look at your face, Gina. You look like a road map. Some of those scars will never go away, especially the ones in your heart."

"Sheila, you know I love you and I believe you mean well but the only thing guns do is end up in the wrong hands. Even if I did try to use it, he would probably take it and use it on me. I do not want to have to choose whether to kill my husband. I will just leave him."

"Okay, Gina, maybe you won't have to use it but at least keep it just in case."

"Girl, I don't know how to use a gun."

"I'll show you. My dad taught me gun safety and everything."

Sheila showed Gina how to use the gun then placed the locked box in her bedside table under some papers.

"Does he ever go in here?"

"No honey. All he does is work, shower, eat, and sleep. He never goes in my drawers."

"Well, even if he does, the box looks like a jewelry box and he can't get in without the key."

"You know it's funny, Sheila, how life is. I mean, here I am sanctified and holy, keeping myself pure for all those years while waiting on the Lord to bless me with a husband, then I end up in an abusive marriage. How did I miss God? Where did I go wrong? I received the Rhema word from the prophet and I believed that my husband was right around the corner."

"He probably was. You just went around the wrong corner, Gina. You married and wolf in sheep's clothing. He dined you and bought you gifts. He was the perfect gentleman. Then he took off his mask on the honeymoon. Well, really he took it off at the reception when he asked you to leave early. Unbelievable! And then to put the cherry on it, he twisted your hand on your honeymoon."

"I can't believe this either. He said the wedding was too long and he told me we should have eloped."

"Lord have mercy, Gina. I would have run right then and filed for an annulment. The marriage would have begun and ended that very same day. But don't beat yourself up, girl. You got yourself into this mess and God will help get you out."

"I know, Sheila, because this is not a marriage. This is torture. When he walks up to me now I just brace myself for the punch or pull or whatever."

"Now you know God did not mean for a woman to be hit on like that. That's not love in any shape or form and you deserve better. You know, Gina, I did some research and found that more women die as a result of domestic violence than those who die from cancer, diabetes, or high blood pressure. I know the statistics are against your survival but you can beat them, my sister. You do not have to die, Gina. God is going to make a way of escape."

Even though she promised Sheila she would leave Greg, two weeks later Gina started to isolate herself from family and friends. She started to feel very depressed when Greg broke his promise again and never went to get help for his abusive behavior. Gina's church attendance was occasional and when she did go to church, she usually sat in the back or in the overflow room just to avoid everyone.

One Sunday after service, Sheila caught up with her.

"Gina, why don't you return my calls?"

"Sheila, I'm sorry. I have just been so busy."

"Gina, is everything alright?"

"Yes, I'm alright."

"It's me, Sheila, that you are talking too. I know the deal, Gina. You don't have to put a mask on with me."

"I will be fine, Sheila, really. I will call you soon," Gina said as she quickly walked away.

As Sheila left the church parking lot to go home, she felt troubled for the rest of the day and could not even eat dinner. Sheila constantly thought of Gina - how her behavior had changed recently and how she had lost so much weight. She looked sick and Sheila wondered what was wrong with her friend. That night Sheila kneeled down to pray.

"My heart is so heavy, Lord. I love you Jesus and I praise you for keeping Gina thus far. You are awesome Lord and I thank you for your protection and for your angles being encamped around those that fear you. Lord, you know all things and nothing is hidden from you. You are able to bring those things that are done in darkness to light. I pray you reveal to me what is going on with Gina. Lead me, Lord, to be a blessing to my sister. I know that you have great things in store for her. You have anointed her to preach the gospel and the enemy is warring against her. She is distant and withdrawn. It is not your burdens that are oppressing her for your yoke is easy and your burdens are light. Deliver my sister, Gina, Lord Jesus. I praise you and I believe you are making a way of escape even now."

Sheila wept for her friend and fell into a deep sleep on the side of her bed. She began to dream. In the dream, it was as if Sheila had a front row seat into Greg and his ex- wife's home. Greg was repeatedly hitting his ex-wife with his fists. The wife fell to the floor unconscious. Greg ran to the bathroom, washed his hand, and cleaned the sink with bleach. He hurriedly broke a back window, removed some valuables from the house, and put them in a locked box in the basement. He then called 911.

73

"I need help right away. Someone has broken into my home, beat my wife, and stole our jewelry. I wrestled with him but he got away."

After giving his address, Greg hung up the phone and looked at his wife as she lay on the floor with blood running from her nose and mouth. She was barely breathing. Greg gave her two final kicks in the head and yelled, "Die!"

Sheila quickly awoke from the dream and she was extremely shaken.

"Oh, my God! Oh, my God! No, Jesus no! Oh God, what is this dream about. Jesus, no!" Shelia shook her head side to side and covered her eyes in disbelief.

"This can't be what really happened to Greg's first wife."

Sheila looked at the clock and it was 5 a.m. It was then impressed upon her spirit to go back to the city where Greg's ex-wife was institutionalized. She heard the Spirit of the Lord say, "Library." Yes, Lord. I will go today. Sheila was convinced in her heart that Greg's physical and verbal abuse would only worsen. I have to help my sister. If he beat his ex-wife like this, he is nuts!

"Lord, lead me to the evidence," she prayed.

Later that morning Sheila showered and got dressed. She searched the internet for libraries in Griffin near the nursing home where Greg's ex-wife lived. She printed the address of the main branch and jumped in her car for the long drive. She put in praise and worship CD, picked up a quick breakfast, and prayed for a safe journey.

"I am in your hands, Lord. You lead me and I will follow."

The drive to the city seemed to take an eternity. Not even sure if the nursing home was in the same city that Greg and his ex-wife lived together, Sheila took a chance. She arrived in the city and went directly to the library. Sheila looked for someone to help her. She didn't want to waste time looking for information when she could just ask for help. Every minute counted. Shelia had no idea what kind of life Gina was living. She could only imagine…

"Good afternoon. May I help you?"

"Good afternoon. I am interested in researching old newspaper articles. Can you point me in the right direction?"

"Yes. I will show you exactly where to go. I have a little spare time. Are you looking for anything in particular?"

Not wanting to reveal that she was trying to see if her best friend's husband is an attempted murderer, she asked about how to search articles for a particular year.

"Can I do that?"

"Sure. I will be glad to help you."

They walked into a large media room and the librarian suggested she take a seat right here in this chair. I will be glad to help you with the microfiche. This is one of our newer models. A microfiche? Shelia questions. Oh my, it has been a while since I've used one so can you refresh my memory? Ok sure. All you have to do is click on the year here and scroll down to the month and date. Let me know if there is anything else I can do to help."

"I will. Thanks again."

Sheila spent several hours looking but found nothing - no stories, no headlines, nothing, not even a wedding announcement.

"Maybe I am going about this the wrong way. Jesus, please help me. I know there is a connection between him and his ex-wife being a near vegetable. Please Lord, lead me. I know you gave me that dream. Where should I go? All these dates and stories could take me a lifetime and I don't have a lifetime. Gina doesn't have a lifetime. I need you now, Lord. Should I leave and go to the police station? I truly thought I heard library in my spirit. You showed me the truth, Lord. I need you."

As if by divine directed, Sheila clicked on an article. The headline read, *Business Man and Wife Attacked by Intruder*.

"What's this?"

Sheila continued to read: *Early Friday evening, Mr. Gregory Gaston, a well-known entrepreneur and businessman, returned home from a business trip and found his wife being attacked by an intruder. After tussling with the suspect for some time, Mr. Gaston was able to scare him off. Unfortunately, his wife had already been severely injured. The police department attributes this incident to other robberies in the area. Mrs. Gaston is in critical but stable condition.*

"He did it! Greg beat his wife, nearly killed the woman and then divorced her. That wasn't a robbery. She was probably trying to leave before he got home. He is a criminal and a serial wife abuser, that's what he is. I have to get to Gina. She is in trouble. God, I hope she will believe me. I hope she will talk to me."

Shelia knew in her heart that Gina was purposely avoiding her, even refusing to have lunch with her on her birthday. Sheila checked the reference articles for updates. The headline of the next article written three months later read, *No Solid Leads on Area Robbery. Due to head and neck injuries, Mrs. Gaston is paralyzed on her right side and cannot speak. Although her husband, Mr. Gaston, has contributed thousands of dollars to the capture of her attacker, no arrests have been made in the case. Mrs. Gaston now resides in Allendale Nursing Home, one of the top centers in the state. Robert McKnight, chief of police and close friend of the Gastons, has officially closed the case.*

Sheila whispered in disbelief, "Case closed? Case closed? Just like that?" Oh yeah, I bet he spent thousands of dollars trying to find the robber. He spent that money paying off the police chief and covering his tracks. Let me print these articles and get out of here."

Driving down the six-lane highway leaving the city, Sheila saw the exit for Allendale Nursing Home. In her spirit, she felt she needed to go there again.

"Lord, I don't know what you have planned but I just have to go see Ms. Gaston one more time."

She quickly got over to the far right lane and exited off the ramp. In the nursing home, Mrs. Gaston was sitting in a wheelchair and gazing out of the window.

"Peace to you, Ms. Gaston. I am praying for you that the Lord will restore to you your complete health."

Ms. Gaston continued to look straight ahead as if she never heard a word.

"You may not remember me. I am Sheila. I visited you over a year ago with my friend, Gina. Gina married your ex-husband, Greg. I just want you to know that the same thing you went through with Greg, Gina is going through now."

Ms. Gaston turned her head toward Sheila with sadness in her eyes and shook her head.

"Ms. Gaston, I want you to know how sorry I am about what happened to you. I know that Greg hit you. It wasn't your fault."

Ms. Gaston looked puzzled.

"Look, if we don't do something, my friend Gina could end up getting seriously hurt too. I believe she is in danger. I need your help. I don't know if you are a Christian but I am and I believe in Jesus Christ and Him being crucified for our sins. He alone is the

Resurrection and the Life. He is also the Lord that is able to heal all of our diseases. I came here, not in my own power, but in the power of the Holy Ghost. Sister Gaston, do you believe that the Lord Jesus can raise you out of this wheelchair and enable you to walk and talk again?"

Ms. Gaston nodded her head yes.

"I believe too, Ms. Gaston. Let's pray."

Ms. Gaston bowed her head and closed her eyes. Sheila prayed and began to praise and thank God in advance for the miracle healing that was about to take place.

"Thank you, God that this miracle is for your Glory and for your honor. Sister, take up your bed and walk in Jesus' name."

Ms. Gaston opened her eyes and touched her face. Her cheek was no longer drooping. She moved the side of her body that had been paralyzed for years. Her left leg touched the floor, then the right leg. Sheila offered her hands out to help Ms. Gaston stand up. With Shelia's assistance, Ms. Gaston leaned out of the chair. Her back straightened and she took small steps, the first steps since the day of the attack. Her balance was unsteady so Sheila supported her as she walked around the room.

"Thank you, Jesus, for this miracle! Now try to talk and give God praise for every step you take. Give him a praise."

With a very low-toned whisper, Ms. Gaston began to praise the Lord.

"Thank you, Jesus. Oh, thank you, Jesus."

Before long she was able to walk without assistance. They rejoiced and praised God until the Holy Ghost fell on Ms. Gaston and she began to speak with other tongues. Her hands were lifted and she danced and shouted all over the dining room. The staff and several residents heard the noise and came to see what was going on. To their surprise, they saw Ms. Gaston walking, running, and giving God glory.

"What happened," asked one of the nurses.

"It's Jesus. He's in the building and He is healing all those who believe."

"I believe."

"I believe, too," said the residents.

Sheila began to pray for everyone who had faith to believe. Miracle after miracle took place. Many were healed and delivered. Later that afternoon before Sheila left, Ms. Gaston was preparing to be discharged from the nursing home and promised Sheila she would go to the police and do whatever she could to be sure justice takes place.

"Give Gina this advice for me. She must have a plan to get away. Greg has a lot of money and he has connections with leaders in high places. She needs to know where she is going and leave quickly. I have to be sure my family is safe and then I will go to the authorities. As usual, he will post bail within hours so I need to have a plan for my family and for myself. One thing is for sure, God has given me another chance at life and I am gonna tell the world of the wonderful and marvelous things He has done for me. I am so glad the Lord sent you back, Sheila. Ms. Gaston began to cry tears of joy.

"He is such a loving God. I sat in that chair for years not being able to talk. I could not even ask someone to take me to the bathroom but look at God. He sent His Word and healed me. I will never be the same. Thank you for being obedient to God. You could have kept driving and gone home but you had an ear to hear what God wanted you to do and you came. And I hear the Lord saying, 'Gina shall live and the enemy will be defeated.' Whatever the devil has planned for her, she will not die. Gina will carry the gospel to save that which was lost. That is for sure."

"Lord I thank you for that word. Ms. Gaston, you haven't been saved two hours and you are already giving a word of knowledge from the Lord! God is good and I thank Him for using you to confirm that my friend will be alright."

"You'd better get going so you can talk to Gina. Don't let her put you off either. Sheila, she needs to know today what a horrible man she is married to."

"Don't worry. I will talk to her as soon as possible. Take care of yourself, Ms. Gaston."

They embraced and prayed for one another one final time then Sheila drove away. Not wasting any time, Sheila picked up her cell phone and dialed Gina's cell number.

"Gina, it's Sheila."

"Hello, Sheila. Why are you calling me on my cell? I am at home."

"This is very private, Gina, and I really need to talk to you today. It will not take very long. Can you come over to my house around seven?"

"No, Sheila, today is not good for me. I have plans."

"This is a life or death situation here, Gina. What time will you be available then?"

Gina noticed the urgency in Sheila's voice as Greg yelled in the background.

"Gina, who is that calling you on your cell? Can't they call us on our home number?"

"Sheila, I will talk to Greg and get back with you. I promise."

"Gina, please be sure to call me."

Sheila knew Gina would not return her call so she decided to take the risk and tell her what she found out over the phone.

"Gina, Greg is not right. He tried to kill his ex-wife and I have proof. Do you hear me?"

Sheila's call had actually interrupted Greg's foot massage.

"Sheila, I will call you back later. Bye."

"Thank you," said Greg. "Now back to the massage, please."

Trying to hide her fear, Gina smiled and continued to rub Greg's feet. Thoughts were going through her mind so fast. *How could this be true? How could Greg have done such a thing? How did Sheila find out?* Greg noticed Gina's behavior.

"What did she want anyway?"

"She wants to see me. She says it is important. Do you think it will be okay for me to run by her house after dinner?"

Surprisingly, Greg agreed.

"But don't be gone all evening."

"Oh, I won't. It shouldn't take more than a couple hours."

"One hour," Greg demanded. "And that includes travel time. Be back here in one hour. You shouldn't be spending a lot of time with a single woman anyway. What do you all have in common? She needs to get a life! You are married, Gina, and have been for a year. Can't she find some single friends to confide in?"

"She has other friends, Greg. It's just that we have been close since elementary school. You know that."

Gina sounded a little too sarcastic for Greg. He slammed his foot down on Gina's fingers and stood up, pressing her hand into the carpet.

"Know what? You are asking me what I know. I know you are not getting smart with me."

"Greg, please. You are hurting me."

81

"It will hurt more if I lift my other leg up and put all my weight on you."

"Please Greg, please."

She tried to free her fingers.

"I didn't mean to offend you. I just wanted to remind you of our friendship that's all. Greg, get off of my hand. If you break my fingers you are going to have to hire a maid and a chef."

"Yeah right," Greg smirked.

He lifted his foot from her hand, walked to the kitchen, and grabbed a cold beer from the refrigerator.

"You know I can afford a maid and a chef if I wanted to. You'd better put some ice on your hand 'cause you ain't getting out of cooking for me tonight."

Gina flexed her fingers and thought to herself, "*Thank God I can move them. My goodness, this right hand is the hand he twisted on our honeymoon. God I know it's you who have not allowed me to have broken bones and I thank you*." To avoid further confrontation, she apologized and grabbed an ice pack from the freezer where she usually kept a good supply for all the bruises and knocks she would get from Greg's abuse.

As if he was a doctor giving orders, Greg said, "Oh yeah, keep it elevated. That should help with the pain."

Gina shook her head behind his back and thought, "*This man is too much and his ways are past understanding. How much longer can I take this abuse?*"

Chapter 10
Enough

After dinner, Gina hopped into her black Escalade. She closed the door and looked at the inside of the car. It was sparkling just like the day Greg brought it home - clean leather seats and not even a smear on the windows. Greg, being a very compulsive neat freak, had the car detailed two to three times a week. Gina gazed toward their home, which was neatly landscaped, and prayed in her heart. *Lord even with all this I am still not happy. I am miserable. I know I made this bed but I want out and I don't know how to get out; not alive anyway.* She started the car and noticed the time. It was 7 p.m. She called Sheila.

"I'm on the way. I only have one hour so let's use it wisely."

"Oh, we will, my sister. I have everything right here for you to look at. I will see you in a few minutes."

When Gina arrived at Sheila's house, she had so many thoughts. *"Do I really want to see this? Lord, I don't think I can handle this right now. Maybe I should come another day".* She turned to leave but Sheila opened the front door and briskly walked toward her.

"Where are you going, Gina? Did you leave something in the car?"

"No, Sheila. I just don't think I am ready for this."

Sheila reached out and grabbed Gina's injured hand.

"Ouch, be careful with that hand," she grimaced.

"Gina, what happened to your hand?"

"Please don't ask, Sheila."

"Look, Gina, God cares about your situation and so do I. Let's pray for your hand. It looks pretty bruised."

Sheila whispered a short prayer and immediately the pain left.

"Thank you, Jesus, for healing my hand. Lord, I praise you. You are so awesome. And thank you, Sheila, for being here when I need you and for speaking God's Word over me. I really needed that. You are a true friend. I love you, sister."

"I love you, too, Gina."

Together they walked into the house.

"I have the information about Greg in the kitchen."

The entire kitchen table was filled with newspaper articles.

"What is this?"

"Well, Gina, I was wondering how I was going to tell you in the little time that we have. First, let me tell you about the dream I had last night. I fasted and prayed for you and asked God to help you and keep you safe. I actually fell asleep on my knees."

Sheila then shared the details of the dream concerning Greg abusing his ex-wife.

"But that was only a dream, Sheila. That can't be true."

"Well, it is, Gina. Will you listen, please? I went back to the nursing home to see Greg's ex- wife but before going there I went to the library and pulled up all these articles written in reference to the night of the attack."

"What? What attack, Sheila?"

"Gina, Greg tried to kill her and set it up to look like a robbery."

Gina read the articles but she was still not convinced.

"How do you know these articles are true, Sheila?"

"Well before I get to that part, didn't Greg tell you that they were divorced first and then Karen had the stroke? Well, according to this article, they were married when the robbery took place and

84

she was placed in a nursing home as a result of her injuries. Why would he lie, Gina?

"I don't know, Sheila, but that still doesn't prove that he did it."

"Well Gina, I have an eyewitness - Karen."

"What do you mean? She can't even talk."

"Well, now she can. God miraculously healed her today and raised her up. She is no longer paralyzed or in that wheelchair. As a matter of fact, she checked herself out of the nursing home today."

"What? Oh, Jesus. How did it happen?"

"Well, we don't have all night, Gina. It's already 7:40 and you said you have to be home by eight. The fact is, God healed her and filled her with the Holy Ghost. She told me that my dream was true and that Greg actually wanted her dead. She was trying to leave him and he went ballistic. She also told me to tell you to make plans to leave Greg but to be careful because he knows a lot of people and he will try to track you down"

Gina put her head on the kitchen table and cried.

"Oh my God! I married a devil. Jesus, Jesus. Lord have mercy."

She fell on the floor in hysteria. Sheila kneeled beside her and tried to console her.

"It's okay, Gina. We all make mistakes, big ones and small ones. Some of them just cost us more. But God promised to bring you out of this. He's here for you, Gina. Even though you married the wrong person, life ain't over. Get up, girl. God is going to fight for you and help you through this. He's been with you this far. He said He wouldn't leave you nor forsake you. He knew what you were going to do before you did it so thank God for grace."

Gina's pain was so deep that she couldn't talk. Her lips moved as if she was trying to say something but the words were not audible.

"I know, Gina, I know. Look, we are going to get you out of there. Don't give up on yourself, girl. God wanted you to know all of this so you could leave before it's too late. You know that God will bring those things that are done in darkness to the light."

"Why couldn't I see all of this before I married him? I just didn't listen. Everyone tried to tell me not to marry him but I was so in love; so convinced that he was my biblical type Boaz. I just knew he was the one Prophet Joel spoke about. I missed God big time and I have been spending the last year of my life in pure torment; in pure torment. Oh Lord, my Lord, my Lord."

Gina began to moan and rock back and forth as she meditated on the error of her decision to marry Greg.

"Gina, you have to get yourself together. You can't change your mistakes. Your mistakes are history. Now live what you preach to other folks. Wipe your tears, sister and get up and make a decision to take whatever you have left in you and live today."

Sheila kneeled on the floor and lifted Gina to her feet.

"Yesterday is gone, honey. Do you hear me? Yesterday is gone and cannot be changed no matter what."

Gina, still in shock as she digests all that Sheila said about Greg and his ex-wife, realized that from day one Greg was not the man God had chosen for her.

"Gina, look at me. You cannot change the fact that you married this demon so let's look forward to the day you won't be married to him; a day that he is behind bars for attempted murder and for physically and mentally abusing you. Karen is going to the authorities real soon but she has to get some things in order first. We need a plan and we don't have time to play around. Come on, girl, let's do this."

"Okay, okay. I hear you. Well, Greg is leaving in the morning for a three-day business trip. I can leave then. Sheila, I do not want to be running all of my life."

"You won't have to. He is going to prison for a long time. So what we will do is get you an apartment out of the city in an anonymous name. You can't call anybody, use credit cards, or anything until he is arrested."

"Well, what about the car. He has that tracking device on all the cars. He can find me anywhere."

"We will have to get you another car."

At that moment there was a knock on the door. They both looked at the clock. It was 8:25 p.m. Oh no. It's Greg. They jumped up.

"Just a minute," said Sheila. "Go to the bathroom and wash your face. I will stall him."

Sheila quickly grabbed all the articles and put them in a drawer while Gina raced to the bathroom, shut the door, and began to pray and wash her face.

"Jesus please don't let this man hurt us. Calm him down right now, Lord."

Sheila opened the door and there stood Greg, grinning and showing his pearly white teeth. Behind that grin, Sheila could see his anger was boiling on the inside.

"Praise the Lord, Sheila. How are you?

"I'm blessed. How about you, Greg?" *You old devil*, she thought.

"I'm good. I just stopped by to check on my wife. I expected her home at eight. You guys must have been having a good time."

"Yes, we did. It was a short visit but we made good use of it. Actually, she is in the bathroom. I will get her for you."

"No that's okay. I won't come in. Just tell her I am waiting for her at home."

"Alright, I will. Take care."

Sheila closed the door and walked toward Gina who was coming down the hallway from the bathroom.

"Girl, he was smiling on the outside but raging on the inside. I do not want to send you home unarmed."

"Sheila, you are not talking about that gun are you?"

"No. In fact, I have repented for giving you that gun. You need to give it back because that is not the Lord's way for you to get out of this. Now tell me what usually happens when you come home late."

"Well, he beats me as soon as my foot hits the door. He tells me I am disrespectful and makes excuses for every lick."

"Well tonight can either be your last whipping or you can be wise as a serpent. It is not going to be easy but you can do it."

"Do what, Sheila?

"Come here."

Sheila walked to her bedroom and pulled out a black negligee with the tags still on it.

"Negligee? What are you doing with a negligee? You are not married yet."

"I know that but I am preparing my wardrobe for when I do get married because faith without works is dead."

"Oh forgive me. I forgot you are a woman of faith. So what is your faith telling you?"

"My faith says you should put this on with these shoes and go home with this on under a raincoat."

"What! You have got to be kidding."

"Well from what you say, he is going to beat you when you get in the door. So, when you get to the door, ring the bell and let him come to the door. You stand outside on the porch with your coat open and let him see you. Then tell him how sorry you are for being late but that it took a little longer to get dressed and that you will make it worth the wait or something like that. Do not, I repeat, do not go in that house. Let him come on the porch and talk. When you are sure in your spirit that his own fleshly desires have overcome those abusive demons in him, then go in the house and yes, for one last time, it won't kill you, as a matter of fact, it may save your life, make love to him. Put it on him!"

"Sheila, you must be kidding."

"No, I am not. Go get dressed now or you may have to go in the nude!"

Gina reluctantly changed into the negligee and high heeled shoes.

"By the way, you owe me for my negligee. It's yours now."

"You are a nut, Sheila. That's why I love you."

They smiled and Gina prepared to leave.

"Call me when he leaves in the morning and I will come over and help you pack."

"I promise. Okay, I hope this works."

"If it doesn't, you'd better call 9-1-1. I don't know why you went this long without reporting him anyway. Well, that's another story, I am sure. Just go and may the Lord lead you tonight."

Gina prayed all the way home.

"Lord, give me wisdom. Please help me through this night. I would rather just go to a hotel and not even go home. Maybe I should. No, then he will cancel the trip looking for me."

She pulled into the driveway.

"Oh well, here we go."

She walked to the door and rang the doorbell.

Greg opened the door.

"Why didn't you use your key?"

Gina smiled and opened the raincoat to reveal her petite figure in the black teddy.

"Well, I thought you might want to take a look at me in the moonlight."

Greg was stunned to see Gina like that.

"Wow!"

"Come out here, Greg. I am really sorry that I am late but it took longer than I thought."

"What took longer?"

He walked out onto the porch and grabbed her around the waist.

"Oh, planning the great things I have in store for you tonight, my loving husband."

"Oh yeah, and what's that," he grinned.

"Well, I thought first I would sing your favorite love song out here on the porch while we dance."

"Out here? Why don't we go inside?"

Gina was not convinced Greg was completely calm. She rubbed his curly hair and started to sing as they danced, kissed, and caressed.

"Gina, I thought you were disobeying me but you were trying to surprise me and I like it, I like it."

"I want you to like it, baby."

Gina continued to sing. Then they walked into the house, up the stairs, and down the long corridor to the bedroom. As Gina thought about Greg's attempted murder of his wife, she imagined her screaming and the pain of her wounds. *"Lord please help me get through tonight. I don't know if I can do this."* Greg noticed the expression on her face.

"What's wrong, Gina?"

"Nothing, my love. I am just thinking about you leaving tomorrow. *Forgive me, Lord,"* Gina says in her mind.

"Well, I told you that you could go with me."

"That's okay. I have plenty to do here at the house."

"So, do I get my going away present, he asked as he kissed her neck.

"Yes, you do."

Gina shut the bedroom door, cut off the lights, and made passionate love to Greg.

Chapter 11

The Getaway

The next morning, Greg kissed Gina on the cheek.

"I'm leaving now baby. I will see you in a few days. I love you."

"I love you too."

Gina rolled over and looked at the clock. It was 6 a.m. She looked out the window and watched Greg put his suitcases into his Mercedes and drive away. She then took a long shower, got dressed, and started to pack. Two hours later Sheila called.

"Is he gone yet?"

"Yes. He left around six."

"What? I thought you were going to call me."

"I didn't want to call you so early. I am packing now."

"Okay, I will be right over."

Sheila arrived 20 minutes later.

"How much are you taking?"

"Well, mainly just my clothes. I will take some appliances but that's about all."

"Do you have money to get an apartment?"

"Yes, I have access to the money. I just don't want him to check the balances and see that I am taking out large sums."

"Well by the time he finds out you will be long gone. Have you told your parents what's going on?"

"No, not yet. I want to go over later today and tell them in person. I don't want to upset them."

"I know, girl, but we need some prayers going up. You haven't made it out yet. Anyway, they need to know that you are going to have to be in hiding until he is arrested."

Sheila's cell phone rang.

"Hello, Sheila, this is Karen. The Lord has allowed me to get things in order. I am on the way to the police station right now to file a report against Greg. I have an attorney who will represent me. Have you talked with Gina?"

"Yes, I did. As a matter of fact, I am helping her pack right now."

"Can I speak to her?"

"Sure. Hold on. Gina this is Karen, Greg's ex-wife. She wants to speak to you."

"Hello, Gina. First I want to thank you for coming to visit me in the nursing home. I enjoyed the singing and the Word of God you shared. Until you all visited me, I had never experienced God that way. As you know, Sheila came back and God miraculously healed me and filled me with the Holy Ghost. I will never be the same."

Gina was happy to hear Karen's testimony. "Well Praise the Lord. God is still healing the sick, and pouring out his spirit on all flesh."

"Yes, he is!" Karen shouted with joy. I plan to be baptized in Jesus name this Sunday as the scripture says. I am so excited to be going down in the water calling on the only name given among men whereby we must be saved." The two celebrate together giving God praise.

"Well, Gina I don't want to hold you long on the phone because I know you are busy."

"If you can give me a few more minutes, I want to talk with you about my horrible abusive marriage to Greg."

Gina anxious to hear Karen's side of the story gives an ear to what she has to say. "Sure take your time. Go right ahead."

"I understand that you are experiencing some of the same abusive things that I lived with. I finally decided to leave him and when he found out about my plans he tried to kill me. I just want you to know that Greg is dangerous and he belongs behind bars. I have been in a nursing home for some time now as a result of his abuse but I thank God for sparing my life, healing my body, and saving my soul! You just don't know. While I was in that nursing home, so many times I tried to talk or write and tell someone what happened but I couldn't. Greg divorced me while I was in the nursing home. He came to see me once and I tried to scream and say get him away from me! He never came back. He told the nurses that I must be upset because I didn't want him to see me in that condition. He left word with the staff to call him immediately if I regained any form of communication no matter the time of day. Oh, he is a devil in every definition. You are doing the right thing by leaving, Gina. Just don't let him catch you packing like he caught me."

Gina was speechless for a moment.

"Thank you, Karen, for telling me this. I know it must have been difficult for you. I have only been married to him for a little more than a year. I can't imagine being married to him for nearly six years."

"Yes, and I stayed because I did not know what else to do. I didn't have a job or money and I felt trapped with no way out. His parents knew he was abusive and covered up for him. They should be punished too as far as I am concerned."

"Yes. Sheila always told me that they knew more than they were saying."

"His mom left the father because he was abusive. Like father like son I guess. Well at least in this case he is like his father"

"Yeah looks like a generational curse that should have been dealt with a long time ago."

"Well, like I told Sheila, I am on the way to the police station with my attorney. It won't be long before the authorities will be looking for him."

"I can tell you now he is in Chicago on a business trip for a few days. Let me give you the name of the hotel where he is staying."

"Thanks, Gina. The authorities will probably wait until he returns before they pick him up."

"Karen, did you all ever have any children?"

"I was eight weeks pregnant when he beat me that last time. I lost the baby."

"Oh, Karen I am so sorry."

"You know I never told him I was pregnant. I suppose the doctors did but I am not sure. I can't remember much about what happened in the hospital because I was so sick but I do remember bleeding heavily and cramping a lot. I guess the baby was not a priority for the doctors since I was so sick. I understand and I am okay with the loss and realize that it was not my fault. I am just glad to be alive and thankful to the Lord for giving me another chance."

"I am too, Karen. Maybe we can talk again soon."

"Yes, that will be great. Let's exchange cell numbers. Gina, you know the police will probably come there looking for Greg."

"Yes, I know."

"Well, give them whatever information they need and feel free to give them my number too."

"I plan to be long gone when he comes back in town."

"Yes, please do."

The next day Gina went to her parents' house to tell them what happened and about her plans.

"I knew it," said Gina's father. "I knew he wasn't right. You had no business marrying that sinner anyway."

"Honey please don't say things like that. It is not making this any easier for Gina. Right now, she needs our prayers and support."

"I am so sorry that I did not listen to either of you or to a whole lot of other people, including my pastor. I was just blind to the truth. Mom, do you remember that dream you had about me a long time ago? You said that I was with this handsome man going into a dark hole. I was smiling but I did not know where he was leading me. Well for the past year, I have been in that dark hole surrounded by demons and evil. I have been tortured mentally and physically. I never thought things could be so bad."

Gina started to cry on her mother's shoulder. Her father touched her head.

"It's okay baby girl. We are going to help you any way we can."

"I am so sorry you guys. Please forgive me for not listening."

"Don't you worry about that. You live and you learn. It could have happened even if you married someone in the church. Abuse is not restricted to people in the world or a particular church denomination, honey. It is a sickness that can happen to anyone at anytime. These days the devil is creeping in everywhere. That's why we have to be careful who we marry and check their background thoroughly. You need to interview everyone and anyone that may know the one you are considering marrying before you fall in love, but that's neither here nor there now. Again, just learn and mature when you fall and get back up again. Gina, you just let us know what we can do to help."

"Well, that's just it. I have to move away just for a little while until he is arrested and sentenced. Even if they arrest him initially, he may post bail. I do not want to be anywhere near him again. I know I have grounds for a divorce."

"Honey you had grounds not to marry him that's for sure. But you can't divorce him unless he committed adultery, said Gina's mom. The scriptures are clear on that. God hates divorce and Jesus' words stating whoever divorces for any reason other than fornication commits adultery according to Matthew 5:32."

"Mom, I can't prove it but I did find women's phone numbers in his drawer. There are plenty numbers in his cell phone and sometimes he smells like perfume that's not mine."

"Well you know that won't hold up in court. We need solid evidence proving that he is an adulterer. Your daddy will help you with that."

"Thanks, dad. I really need to get going. Here is my new address. I can only call you. You can't call me because Greg may trace the calls. I will be leaving in the morning. Greg is due back tomorrow evening. The truck should be pulling out about 8 a.m. and I will be right behind it. I will call you when I get there. Sheila is going to help me get settled in."

"Okay. We love you."

They say a prayer and kiss Gina goodbye.

The next morning, the truck pulled off with Gina's belongings and headed toward her new apartment. Sheila was at the apartment unpacking. Gina put some bags into her car and answered her cell phone. It was Sheila.

"Hey, Gina. Are you finished with those last few bags yet?"

"Almost. I just have to empty out my nightstand and get a few other things."

"Well hurry up."

"I am, girl, but relax. I don't expect him back until tonight. I'm okay."

"Alright see you in a few."

Gina walked into the house and took a sigh of relief.

"Lord I thank you that this is about over. I can finally leave this man and start fresh."

Just then, she heard the sound of a car door closing and looked out the window.

"Oh no. It's Greg! He's early! Jesus, Jesus! Oh, sweet Jesus. Oh Lord Jesus."

Gina ran and hid in a closet. When Greg walked in, he noticed pieces of furniture missing.

"Gina, what's going on here? Gina where are you?"

He walked through the house calling Gina's name louder and louder. He hit the wall hard with his fist.

"I know you are not trying to leave me, Gina? I know you are in here so you might as well come out."

Hiding in the closet, Gina began to shake in fear. Her hands could barely hold the door closed. Greg walked by the closet and into the kitchen and then Gina's cell phone rang. As she reached into her purse to silence the phone, Gina began to pray, "*No weapon formed against me shall prosper and every tongue that rises up against me God shall condemn. When my enemies come up against me the Lord will lift up a standard against them.*"

Greg opened the closet door and pulled Gina out by her hair. He threw her across the floor.

"What do you think you are doing? You stupid woman," he cursed. "Are you trying to leave me? Are you serious?"

He slapped and kicked Gina as she crawled on the floor trying to avoid his punches.

"Greg, it's over. I can't take it anymore. You don't love me. Just let me go. Please let me go."

"Go where? You're just going to come in here and pack up my stuff and leave? I know that old witch, Sheila, had something to do with this. I told you I was going to get some help. Didn't I? Didn't I?"

"You can still get help, Greg. I just need to go that's all."

"Well let me tell you something, Mrs. Gina. My first wife tried this stuff and it didn't work. She would have been better off staying with me but no, she was tired. I gave her everything she could ever want."

Greg was thinking out loud as he choked Gina. "I told her. I begged her not to leave. But she wouldn't listen and now she is in a nursing home because she just wouldn't listen."

Gina gasped for air as her small hands pulled at his large masculine hands. Her fingers were no match for the tight grip he held around her neck. He jerked Gina's neck and released her. Gina coughed and took a deep breath. She gasped and crawled backward on the floor. Not to dare reveal to him that Karen was healed and well, she tried to change the subject.

"Please, Greg, I don't want to talk about your ex-wife now. We are two different people."

"Yes. You are two women who are blind and can't see a good man right in front of you. I know one thing, I bet she wishes she had not tried to leave me and you are going to wish the same thing."

He slapped her again.

"Greg, please stop. I don't know what happened to you after we got married but you changed like Dr. Jekyll and Mr. Hide."

"What do you mean woman? I always felt like slapping your butt. I was tired of you and your Jesus mess so I got baptized just to shut you up, hoping to get into your pants. When I saw that you wouldn't give it up, I just kept on seeing other women and I still do."

"You are no good, Greg. I hate the day I met you."

"Well, you are gonna hate this day too. I am going to kill you!"

Greg continued to beat Gina with his fists. He threw her across the room. Gina hit her head on the china cabinet and blood flowed heavily down her face. He repeatedly beat her for about 20 minutes and only stopped because of exhaustion. By now, Gina's vision was blurry because of the blood that covered her eyes. Large clots of blood poured from her nose; her lips were swollen, and her gums were bleeding from the force of his fists against her teeth. She could barely walk because of the traumatic force of the punches to her head. However, she managed to make it to the bedroom and lock the door. She pulled a table in front of the door. Greg followed her to the room yelling.

"You will die tonight and I don't care what happens to me as long as you die. I am the man here. This is my house and you and the house belong to me!"

As Greg shoved on the door, Gina remembered the gun in her nightstand and recalled Sheila's voice, *"A woman has to do what a woman has to do. Don't let me regret that I did not turn him in. It may come down to you or him. Make the right choice, Gina."* Fright filled Gina's heart as she looked at the drawer knowing that the loaded gun was there. She had within her reach the power to end it all—all the abuse, all the pain. *I can just empty the gun on him and*

101

it will be self-defense, she thought. *If I don't do something, he is going to kill me this time.*

In desperation, Gina prayed, "I am so sorry for being disobedient, Lord. I knew he wasn't saved. I was stupid, stupid to marry him. I should have known those demons in him would try to kill me. Everyone told me he wasn't the one. He never loved you and therefore he had no rights to me. Please forgive me for marrying this man. I want to live Jesus. If I ever needed your Spirit, I need it now. I want to live and not die. All souls are yours, God. I don't want to kill this man." She continued to pray. "Please deliver me from the enemy that is warring against me."

Gina opened the drawer and pulled out the box. As she searched frantically for the key to unlock the box, Greg was nearly tearing down the bedroom door. She grabbed the box, ran in the bathroom, and locked herself inside. She clearly heard a voice say very urgently, "*Be still and know that I am God.*" Another voice said, "*Kill him or he will kill you.*" Gina had nothing to block the bathroom door. It would only take seconds for Greg to unlock the door. "*Don't do it, Gina,*" the voice said. "*Stand still and see the salvation of the Lord. You will not have to kill him. This battle is not yours, it's mine.*" Gina knew it was the spirit of the Lord.

Greg lunged through the door with anger and hatred in his eyes. He was breathing rapidly as beads of sweat rolled down his face. He no longer looked like a man. He looked like a beast with red eyes, fully possessed. Gina thought, "*Well, if I am not to fight, then I guess I am supposed to die.*"

Gina held the gun to her side as Greg approached. He was within inches from her body. She screamed to the top of her lungs, "Jesus, save me!!"

102

Greg immediately stopped, grabbed his chest, and fell to the floor. He was shaking. He let out a loud groan and said, "It's my heart. Oh my God what is happening to me," he asked as he fell.

Gina crawled over to him.

"Gina, please help me."

She reached for his cell phone to call for help.

"This is the 9-1-1 operator. What is your emergency?"

"Please send an ambulance right away. My husband just collapsed. It may be his heart."

Chapter 12

A Way of Escape

"Ashes to ashes, dust to dust. Naked we came into this world and naked we shall return."

At the graveside service, the preacher prayed a final prayer before laying Greg to rest. One woman at the funeral whispered to another, "You know, he was only 42 years old; healthy fellow. He ate right, exercised and everything. The doctors say his heart just got off beat and he died. Poor Gina. She has been through a lot. I heard that he beat her the whole time they were married. This time he hit her so hard his heartbeat got irregular and couldn't take it anymore. He just dropped dead right there. Now you know that is something. You just never know where death is. That's why it's best to live right."

"Amen, it sure is. What do you think she is going to do now?"

"I don't know honey. I heard he was rich and had a lot of stores all over the United States and overseas. She got all that money and the businesses too."

Gina left the gravesite with her parents and Sheila at her side. As she walked toward the car, she looked at Sheila with tears in her eyes.

"You know, I am going to consecrate myself unto the Lord for six months; nothing but prayer, fasting, and the Word. I have to build myself back up. God allowed me to live through this horrible marriage and He didn't allow the devil to kill me. He fought for me and gave me another chance and I am so grateful."

"I know, Gina. I am grateful too. I'm grateful that the Lord fought for you and delivered you from the enemy."

"Hallelujah. Thank you, Jesus. That could have been me in that casket but God protected me. He made a way of escape for me. The Lord fought my battle."

Onlookers noticed her praise, and, having no knowledge of her situation or her personal story, began to murmur.

"No, she ain't praising God at her husband's grave. Shame on her!"

"Can you believe that? Now you know that ain't right. No matter what happened that just ain't right."

Chapter 13
African Missionary

Six months later, Gina completed her consecration. She was revived and full of the Holy Ghost. The Lord had spoken to her and called her to go to Africa. While waiting to board her flight at the airport, she and Sheila said their goodbyes.

"Well, Sheila, I guess this is it my buddy, old pal, my sister."

"Yeah, girl, I know. Call me as soon as you get there, okay. Go fulfill your destiny, woman of God. Turn Africa upside down!"

"Okay, I will. I love you, Sheila."

They shared a smile and a final hug.

"I just thank the Lord for His healing power and restoration. Now I must continue the work He has given me. I know there are many souls in Africa in need both physically and spiritually and I am expecting God to open doors for the Gospel to be preached."

Gina spent a year in Africa preaching the gospel, with signs and wonders following. Many were saved and healed by the mighty hand of God.

Back in the United States, the phone rang at the home of Gina's pastor.

"Hello."

"Well praise the Lord, Pastor Johnson. This is Bishop Smith. I know you haven't heard from me in about two years now but I am blessed. You know soon after I preached at your church the Lord sent me to Africa as a missionary and I have been here ever since. The Lord is blessing so much that mere words cannot tell it all. God is so awesome!"

"Bishop, that's great to hear. You know one of my members is there working as a missionary also. Her name is Evangelist Gina Gaston."

"Yes, Pastor, well that's another reason I am calling. I heard that there was a powerful woman of God here from America and that she was a member of your church. I wanted to invite her to speak at one of our meetings and I thought I would get a recommendation from you first."

"Oh, yes, praise God. She will be a blessing to your people. God is using her mightily."

"Well, I will take your word and trust your judgment. I will invite her and perhaps we can support one another in ministry as the Lord leads.'

"That will be fine, Bishop."

"You know, pastor, I never told you this but after my wife died I asked God for a new companion and He showed me a beautiful woman's face. She was working very diligently to win souls for Christ. In this vision, I saw you waving to me and saying, 'Come over here. The fulfillment of God's promise is over here. Come and see your bride.' I believed that somehow my new wife and you were connected but I didn't know how exactly. Then you invited me to preach at your church. That night of the service I was expecting to see her face. The Lord specifically told me that my wife would be at the service and that she would be serving me if she was obedient. I did not understand what that meant and, well I did not see her face at the service or after the service. I was very disappointed. Not long after that I decided to leave for Africa and have been here ever since. I have had another vision of her since then except she was weeping bitterly and the Lord instructed me to pray for the weeping woman. I did and still do pray for her. God has been good but it has been hard laboring without a wife. But praise God He has kept me."

Pastor Johnson was silent for a moment as he reminisced on the night of the revival and his sharing with Gina what he felt the Lord had in store for her at the service. His words came back to him so clearly. *Gina, I believe that God has something special for you and many others in this service.* Then it was clear to him what God wanted to do and his mind raced. *What? It was Gina! I don't believe it. Gina was supposed to be at church but she didn't come that night.*

"Pastor Johnson, are you okay man? Sounds like you were in deep thought."

"Oh yeah man, sorry. I'm okay. Go ahead and finish. What were you saying?"

"You know, Pastor, I have gone on a few dates with a missionary from England. I like her, she is beautiful, mature in the Lord, and has a kind spirit but I am just not feeling a connection. The woman in my vision looks nothing like her and, well, will you pray with me? I really need some prayer about the whole thing concerning this relationship and this woman who I believe lives somewhere in this world and is my wife. I do not want to keep dating this other woman when I know she is not the one for me. I do not want to waste her time or mine. She is actually the only woman I have dated since my wife died. I poured myself into my ministry and into spending time with Lord. Not only that man, but the bond between my wife and I was so strong you know. And, and I just couldn't..."

Pastor Johnson interrupted, "Yes I know man. I can only imagine how hard it's been for you but you are still here and God hasn't forgotten His promise to you."

"Pastor, you are right and I believe it is time for me to be married again. I want to share my life with someone and only that someone ordained for me. I am not hearing the Lord say that the woman I am seeing is my wife and I don't want to mislead her. Since I really believe that you are somehow connected to the wife God has ordained for me, I am planning to come and visit your church again soon; not to preach, just to visit. I have been praying but it seems that the Lord is silent. As you know, it is at moments of silence like this that many people miss out on their blessing. I am determined to believe God and wait for the manifestation of His promise."

"Bishop, you are so right. My friend, my brother, the only thing I have to say to you is continue to pray. I have a feeling that God is about to break the silence."

Pastor Johnson smiled as he thought of Gina being in Africa and soon meeting Bishop Smith.

"Let's pray."

After the prayer, Pastor Johnson asked Bishop Smith "When is the revival?"

"Our revival is this weekend. I would like for Evangelist Gaston to be our keynote speaker. Bishop Slate had to cancel due to personal reasons. Then one of our fellow ministers mentioned Evangelist Gaston. Do you have contact information for her?"

"Sure. Here are her home and cell numbers. She is a very busy lady and she travels often. I sure hope she is available on such a short notice."

Bishop Smith wrote the numbers on his notepad and thanked Pastor Johnson.

"I will have my secretary call and invite her."

"It was good hearing from you, Bishop Smith. Will you do me one favor? As soon as you receive your answer to your prayers and you meet your wife, will you let me know how things are going?"

"Wow, Pastor. You act like it is going to be soon."

"Well, Bishop, you never know. You just never know."

They laughed.

"Well, of course, I will, Pastor. You be blessed."

Later that day, Bishop Smith's secretary informed him that Evangelist Gaston had accepted the invitation.

"She will be flying in from another engagement and will arrive at service time. Unfortunately, she will not be able to meet with you prior to the service. However, she and her armor bearer will meet with you after service."

Bishop thought to himself, *Hmm, wise woman. She will meet with me with her armor bearer. Wise indeed.*

Bishop Smith's thoughts were interrupted when the woman he has taken out a few times called.

"Hello, Tony. This is Carol. How is everything going with plans for the revival? I know you were trying to find another speaker."

"Yes, Carol. Actually, the Lord has worked everything out. Evangelist Gaston will be our speaker. I have not heard her before but she is highly recommended. Are you still able to come?"

"Sure, I will be there."

She paused, hoping Bishop Smith would ask her out to dinner. She believed the brief courtship would end in marriage and that she would be the perfect first lady.

"Is there anything I can do to help you, Tony?"

"No, no. Everything is taken care of. You just come and be blessed and I will see you Saturday at church."

His secretary walked into his office just as he hung up the phone.

"Another date with Carol I presume?"

"Actually no, Mrs. Ears," he teased.

"You know Bishop, she is a nice lady but I don't think she is the one for you."

"Why do you say that?"

"Well, I get the impression that she only wants you for your money and your position. She seems to be that type."

"Oh, you think so?"

"Yes, I do. I mean I could be wrong but it sure seems that way."

"Well, I haven't bought her anything at all except dinner. I don't think she can get rich off of a meal do you?"

"Okay, Bishop. You know how leeches are. They start off with little small sucks till they drain you dry!"

"I'll remember that. Thanks for the advice."

On the day of the revival service, Gina's plane arrived as planned. She called Bishop Smith's office and told the secretary that she had landed and, as expected, would be arriving late.

"Oh, that's fine. I'm glad you had a safe flight. I will tell Bishop you are still coming. We look forward to seeing you shortly."

An hour and a half later, Gina arrived at the church. She was escorted to the pulpit where she kneeled at her chair to pray before being seated. Bishop Smith was at the podium leading a worship song, *My heart's desire is to love you, Jesus, and to serve you till the day I die. You are worthy. You are worthy, Jesus. You are worthy of my sacrifice.* The interpreter sang the lyrics in the local language. Gina joined in the worship thinking what a beautiful song and perfect for setting the atmosphere for a powerful move of God. After the selection, it was time for the Word of God. Bishop Smith turned to get a glimpse of Gina but couldn't see her face because the usher was serving water and asking for the Evangelist's bio.

"We are thrilled to have Evangelist Gina Gaston here. Please allow me to introduce her."

The usher passed the bio to Bishop and he began to read.

"Evangelist Gina Gaston is from the United States, a native of Atlanta, Georgia. God called her into the ministry at an early age..."

He completed the bio, looked back at Gina, and invited her to the podium. As he stretched out his right hand toward Gina, to his surprise the vision of his bride was right in front of him. Gina's hair was slightly pulled up and flowed in the back. Her smile was angelic and her eyes sparkled. Bishop's right hand held her right hand. He lifted his left arm towards her shoulder and, with a distant hug, he said, "Welcome. We are glad to have you."

"Thank you," Gina said.

As their hands separated, they both felt a tingling sensation at the tips of their fingers. Bishop sat down in amazement and his mind began to race. *"That face, Lord; that face. How can it be? That's her. That's her."* He stared at Gina in awe as the usher gave him a glass of water. He quickly grabbed the water and drank it down straight.

"Oh Jesus! Is she married now? It's been so long since you gave me that vision. Am I too late?"

He heard the spirit of the Lord say, "No, my son. You are not late."

Gina had no clue about what Bishop was thinking. She opened the Bible and preached a powerful message on worship.

113

Signs and wonders followed. The lame walked and deaf ears and blinded eyes were opened. After ministering, Gina was escorted off the pulpit. Bishop Smith sent a message to Gina reminding her that they were to meet after service. Gina was exhausted but agreed to meet. She and her armor bearer walked into Bishop Smith's office and took a seat.

"Praise the Lord, Evangelist, and how are you, my sister?"

"Praise the Lord, Bishop."

"Powerful message. The Lord really used you tonight."

"That is our prayer - to be a living sacrifice for the Lord. Please pray for me that I continue to stand in His will because it is not easy."

"I sure have... I mean I sure will pray for you."

Bishop stumbled over his words knowing he had been praying for Gina for years.

"Well, I know that the hour is late. I would just like to thank you for accepting our invitation. You were highly recommended by your pastor and many others."

"My pastor? You talked to Bishop Johnson?"

"Why yes. He and I are friends."

"Well isn't this is a small world," she said. "I appreciate your considering me and if I can be of further assistance, please call."

"Yes, I will. Are you in Africa with family?"

"No, I came alone. I am a widow. My parents and siblings are in the states and I decided to come here after my husband died."

"Oh, I am so sorry to hear that. I lost my wife to breast cancer about seven years ago. It is very hard when you lose a spouse. Were you married long?"

"No actually. Just a little over a year. He had heart problems."

"That must have been difficult."

"Yes it was and actually it is a long story. But the Lord brought me through," Gina said as she thought of the abusive relationship. "But I have been here for about a year now and God is allowing me to help others despite my past pain."

A year, Bishop thinks to himself. *She has been here a whole year and I didn't even know it.* "Well thank the Lord. I know you are probably hungry. Would you like us to get you something to eat?"

Oh no. I am fine. I just need rest. I am too tired to eat. I can eat in the morning"

"Okay. Let's have breakfast then."

Gina looked a little surprised.

"Oh no. You don't have to do that. Really."

"I want to. I'd love to share some old memories with you. I used to come to Atlanta a lot to preach and teach. As a matter of fact, I came to your church right before I came to Africa. It was in June a couple years ago I believe. You were having a Holy Ghost Miracle revival. Were you there?"

Gina looked at Bishop and had a quick flashback of the night she did not go to the revival so she could spend that evening with Greg - the night he proposed.

"No I did not make it that night but I heard the Lord really blessed."

"Yes, He did. Were you out ministering at that time?" Bishop asked, recalling that God said she would serve him that night.

"Well no. I just had some last-minute plans."

"Hmm. Those must have been some kind of plans."

"They ended up being just that. Gina replies sarcastically. "But I am sorry I missed your preaching."

Gina stood up as if she was ready to go.

"Maybe I can come to one of your services," Gina said.

"Of course, Evangelist. Anytime."

"Well I guess we will say goodnight now," Gina said.

"Okay. Thanks again to both of you. By the way, I'd like to finish telling you about my Atlanta story if you will have breakfast with me."

"Ok, that will be fine. Here is my card."

"Thank you. Is 9 a.m. okay?"

"Yes, that is fine. See you then."

Gina and her armor bearer walked out of the Bishop's office.

"What was that all about," said the armor bearer.

"I am not sure but something tells me I am going to find out tomorrow."

After the women left his office, Bishop Smith smiled in amazement.

"Look at you, Jesus. You have brought this woman to me all the way from Atlanta. You are so awesome. No one but you could have done this and I pray she receives me. She is so beautiful and anointed; so beautiful inside and out. She was here for a year and I did not even know it but thank you for the appointed time. Thank you, Lord. Thank you. Thank you, Lord."

He picked up the phone to call his friend, Bishop Johnson. He could hardly wait to tell him about Gina.

"Hello, Bishop Johnson? Bishop Smith here. Sorry for calling you at an odd hour but I just had to tell you how God met us here in a mighty way."

"Well good, good. Did Evangelist Gaston make it to the service?"

"Yes, she did. I was actually happily surprised to finally meet her."

"Finally," Bishop Johnson asked as if to prompt him to tell the whole story.

"Yes. I have been looking and waiting for my wife for seven years."

"Well, seven years is a long time to wait, my friend. You sound like Jacob when he waited for Rachael."

"Yes, you are right but I am not going to wait another seven. You can believe that."

They laughed together.

"No man, we will not be fooled this time. Our eyes are wide open to the enemy's devices."

"Well, I am glad to hear that."

"So when did you find out that Gina was the one that God had spoke to me about," asked Bishop Smith. "And why didn't you tell me?"

"Look, I did not put it together until you called and told me she was going to speak at your church. By that time, I felt like you should see her and know within yourself if she was the one."

"Oh, I see. So that's why you made that comment before we got off the phone. Ok. I forgive you. I mean I have to."

They laughed again.

"She wasn't at the revival service that I preached for you was she?"

"No, my brother, she was not there and all I can say is that she was supposed to be. She will have to tell you the rest."

"Alright, alright. Can you at least tell me if she came at all that night?"

"If I recall correctly, you went out of one door and she came in another; just minutes apart."

"Was she alone?"

"Now that's two questions."

"She wasn't, was she? Now I know why she was weeping. She was with a man that was sent by the enemy as a distraction; at least that is what I hear the Spirit saying to me. Well, I guess on tomorrow I will find the answers to my questions."

"Bishop, I will be praying for you both. I know you must have a lot of questions but Gina is the only one that can answer them."

"You're right. Well, thanks for being obedient and inviting me to preach that year. You did your part. Now I need to find out why Gina wasn't obedient. She should have been there at the service."

"I know, I know," said Bishop Johnson. "You can't turn back time man. Just live in the now."

"I will. Thanks. We will talk soon."

"Alright. Be blessed."

Chapter 14

The Truth

"Are you pretty hungry, Gina?"

"Actually I am, Bishop. Because of my schedule, I haven't had a decent breakfast all week; just fruit or yogurt or something quick."

"Well, you should like this place. They have all sorts of meats, omelets, fruit, grits, pancakes, you name it."

"Okay, that's enough. You are making me hungrier."

They laughed.

"You know, Gina, I wish I had the patience to wait until after we eat to tell you my story but I just can't hold my peace."

"Well don't hold it. I like stories, especially when you talk about home."

"Well, here it is. Once upon a time, there was a man of God who lost his wife as a result of breast cancer. Three years after she died, God promised to bless him with a wife. One day while he was in prayer, the Lord showed him a vision. In the vision, he saw Bishop Johnson's face. Bishop Johnson was saying, 'Come and preach. Come and preach.' And then he saw a beautiful woman smiling with the glory of the Lord shining on her face. She was serving the homeless and visiting the sick, and preaching the gospel. Then the voice of the Lord spoke and said 'She is your wife. You two shall become one and serve me. Many shall you bless with my gospel.' The man asked God, 'Where is she, Lord? Where can I find my wife?' God answered and said, 'She shall come to you in due season.'

That very next day the man received a call from Bishop Johnson inviting him to come and preach at his Holy Ghost miracle revival. Bishop Johnson said God was directing him to have the service that week and that specific man should be the speaker. He asked if the man could come on that Friday. Without hesitation, the man accepted the invitation because he remembered the vision he had the previous day. On the afternoon of the service, the man of God asked the Lord if he would see his promised wife that night. God said, 'She has been asked to serve tonight. Pray for her obedience to my voice.' The man promised God he would pray for her and immediately began to do so. He started to pray for his wife and asked God to help her discern good from evil and to be able to hear and obey God's voice. But the prayer was ended abruptly due to an emergency phone call. The emergency held up the man until it was time for the church service that night.

The service was blessed and highly anointed by God. Many people received physical healing and the man later received word from Bishop Johnson that his church members were still being blessed. Mortgages were paid off, people received cars, and souls were added to the Kingdom. But the preacher left the church that night disappointed. He was convinced in his heart that he would meet his bride-to-be that night because God specifically told him that she would serve him. So, during the fellowship dinner after service, he looked at the faces of each of the servers and hostesses but he never saw her face. He asked the pastor if there were any more servants but he was told there were not. He even stayed until the last guest left the building, hoping and waiting to see his bride. She never came. He went home that night feeling depressed and even foolish and wondered within himself how he could have missed God. 'I must be so lonely that I am delusional,' he thought.

'I am going to get my mind on you God and off of being married because this is about to drive me crazy.' So, he planned to go to Africa as a missionary and has been here ever since.

That was nearly four years ago. To this day he is still single. Just the other day he spoke to a friend and asked him about a certain woman – one of his members - and her ministry. Her pastor spoke very highly of her and said she was a great supporter of his ministry. Her name is Evangelist Gaston. She was assigned to lead praise and worship that night long ago at the churches Holy Ghost revival, and she was supposed to serve the ministers during the fellowship dinner after service. Before ending the call, the friend told this man to call him as soon as he finds out who his wife is. This man heard what his pastor friend said but he did not make any connection at all between this woman and the woman in his vision. On the recommendation of his pastor friend, the man invited the evangelist to preach at one of his services."

Gina's eyes began to water and she picked up a napkin to wipe her tears. Bishop Smith continued talking and gently placed his hand on Gina's hand.

"You know what? It wasn't until the man introduced the evangelist to the congregation from the pulpit and looked upon her face that everything came together - the vision of Bishop Johnson saying come preach; her face; and then Bishop Johnson telling him to call him as soon as he finds out who his wife is. It was in that moment when he shook her hand and placed her Bible on the podium that he knew in his heart that this was his promised wife. 'God, that is my wife,' he thought. And then to sit down and hear her preach such a powerful word and see how the Lord used her, he was in awe. Gina, to conclude my story, I must say that I am the man of God who so longed for his wife for years. And your face is the face in my vision. To sit here now and see with my natural eyes what I once could only see in the spirit is amazing. Just to see you, Gina, was worth every battle, every obstacle, every lonely night, and the entire wait. This is truly a miracle from God."

He looked at Gina intensely. She took a deep breath.

"Gina, I just hope you see what I see and hear what I hear."

"Yes, I see what you see and indeed this is a miracle. You see, that woman had prayed and waited so long for her husband. She became discouraged and frustrated with the whole process of sewing and reaping. When she was in prayer, God spoke to her and said your season shall come. God confirmed His promise through a prophet who told her specifically that God had heard her prayer and that she would soon meet her husband. He also warned her concerning the enemy's deception and the importance of being obedient to God. The woman did not see then the whole picture but now she sees clearly what happened."

Gina looked down in shame and continued her story.

"Shortly after the prophecy was received, this woman met a man who was not saved. Thinking he was the promised one, she began to witness to him and to date him. The man eventually got baptized in water and started going to church. He was a very wealthy man who had been previously married and divorced. Bishop Johnson and many others advised her not to continue the relationship but her heart was being drawn closer and closer to him.

The night of the miracle revival was one of the hardest spiritual battles she had ever fought. She was asked by this man to meet with him because he was leaving the next morning for a business trip. He had given hints that he may ask her hand in marriage. She was also asked by her pastor to serve at church that same evening. She prayed and asked God what she should do and

God told her to go to church. But she disobeyed God and asked God to forgive her. She promised she would make it up to the church by serving at another time.

She wrestled in the spirit realm with the demonic influence the man had over her but still, she made deals with God, reminding Him of how many times she had gone to church, how long she had labored in the vineyard, and how this was now her time. So, she went to dinner instead of going to the revival service. The man proposed to her that night and she accepted. On the night of their wedding, he physically abused her. He continued to abuse her throughout their marriage. After a little more than a year of marriage, she finally decided to leave him after obtaining proof that he had abused and nearly killed his first wife. She knew then blinders were on her eyes and that she could not see the truth before.

One day while the husband was away on a trip, she prepared to leave. As she was packing the last or her belongings, he came home early. He beat her for nearly two hours. While attempting to get away, she remembered she had a gun that was given to her by a friend for protection. She wrestled with the thought of shooting him but decided against it and opted to pray that God would deliver her from the immediate danger of the situation. As he lunged for her a final time, he grabbed his chest, fell to the floor, and cried out for help. The woman called 9-1-1. The ambulance arrived but he died on the way to the hospital. He suffered a heart attack.

After his burial, the woman consecrated herself before the Lord for six months of fasting and praying. She was then called to Africa by God and she has been here for a year. You know what? The funniest thing happened last night when I got home. I looked through an old purse and in it was the prophecy I was given years ago. I had written down what I could remember. One of the last things that was said to me was that my husband and I would minister together in Africa. I had forgotten all about that part of the prophecy until I read it last night. Bishop, that woman is me."

"Oh Gina, what made you look at the prophecy last night?"

"Well, when we shook hands last night, I felt the anointing so strong. It made me wonder what that was all about. Another thing is the way you looked at me. You looked at me like you knew me, which made me wonder whether we had met before. Being in your presence last night felt right for a lack of a better word."

"Yes it did, Gina. And now feels right, too. Now, what did God say about Africa?"

"He said that my husband and I would minister together in Africa."

"Look at God!" Bishop said. "He told you that years ago and here we are in Africa."

"Yes, we sure are. Now that is something," she replied.

Bishop rested his chin in his hand and gazed into Gina's eyes.

"I am really amazed at this, Gina. You know, I got very little sleep last night because I spent so much time thanking and praising God for bringing us together. Even though I have just met you I feel like I have known you for a long time. In these few minutes, you have shared with me your heart, your secrets, your struggles, and I want you to know I admire you for that. I hope I am not being too straight forward."

The waitress came to the table to take their order.

"Bishop, I appreciate your honesty and no, you are not being too straight forward. You make me very comfortable to talk and put the pieces of the puzzle together. I was hungry but now, for some reason, I am not."

"Me neither."

"It must be all the excitement but we should eat a little something."

"As hard as you preached last night, I know you need some nutrition to replenish yourself," Bishop said as they exchanged smiles. "Gina, why did you make me wait so long, woman?"

"Well, I am sorry. I did not know where you lived," she laughed.

"You know, I was just getting ready to seek the Lord again for a wife. It has been years since I have sought Him in reference to marriage. After coming to your church that night, it really hurt my ego that I missed God like that being the prophet that I am. I just knew my wife-to-be would be there. You! My wife. How does that sound to you?" He paused. "It almost sounds strange to actually be talking about you being my wife and we just met."

"That's okay," she reassured. "Let's just call it faith; calling those things that are not as though they were."

"And I am definitely calling a whole lot of things to come to pass real soon. And I pray that we can spend some time getting to know each other. I mean God already knows us and our individual likes and dislikes but I know it would help me to know more about you on a personal level. How is your schedule?

"Well I am pretty busy most days and that is on purpose. I try to keep myself occupied."

"Is there any room for adjustments at least twice a week?"

"Oh, I think I can handle that."

For the next few months, Bishop Smith and Evangelist Gina talked to each other or saw each other every day.

Chapter 15
Love Will Wait

This is a beautiful day, isn't it, Gina" Bishop asked as they walked through the park. "The sky is such a beautiful blue color today and the sun is so bright. Gina, I have a question for you."

They walked over to a bench and took a seat. Bishop Smith gently took both her hands into his.

"How long do you think we should date? You know I teach my people that dating is for brief periods. Gather all your information, go pray, and ask God questions. Ask Him if this person is the one for you. If not, move on. But see, I knew you were the one years ago. I really do not need God to confirm that your character was a match for mine. He knew that when He told me you were my wife. I know you are a woman of God and that's the most important thing but let's face it, every woman of God does not have the character to be my wife. So I guess what I am trying to say again is how much longer do you want to get to know me?"

He looked into her eyes.

"I know all I need to know at this point. As you know, the car remains in the showcase until purchased. No test driving."

"Now you know I know that," Bishop replied with a little smirk on his face. "I know the Word now. It is better to marry than to burn but one thing is for sure, just because you are burning doesn't mean it's time to be married. If I had only wanted to stop the burning, I would have missed you."

"So are you saying you were going to get married before?" Gina asked in surprise.

"I have been introduced to more preachers, evangelists, and ushers than you can count on your hand. It's not that any of them were not beautiful but they were not for me. They were not who God promised me. Yes, there was a time when I said I would go ahead and date seriously and find a wife. Recently the Lord said no, she's not the one. Of course, I've gone through lonely days and nights. I cried out to God, 'When, Lord, when, when?' I know you may find this hard to believe but I was actually planning to go back to the States to look for you. Don't ask me where I was going but I was going to start with your pastor. I believed he could somehow connect me with you.

"You are right. I do find that hard to believe. You were just going to go back to the States looking for this nameless face?"

"I did it once and I would do it again if it meant I would find you."

"You are determined, aren't you?"

"Yes, I am."

"Well, I would just like to know how you were able to keep all the women away."

"Easy! Whenever I would get up to preach, I would just tell the congregation that I was single and waiting; not interested in dating and that I was drawing closer to God and He was my only companion. So people stopped trying to set me up and the sisters backed off a bit. But then rumors started and people would say, 'Bishop must be impotent or depressed.' I even heard some say I must be gay. When people don't understand, sometimes they feel they have to find a reason to explain a certain thing. None of those reasons are true, Gina, believe me. I just thank God for keeping me."

He put his arm around her shoulder.

"I must say this. I don't need to date you anymore," he said leaning closer and moving Gina's hair from her face. "It is not wise for me to date you anymore. I am too close to the fire to date you anymore. Do you get what I am saying? I know that I know that I know that you are the one for me. I just dated you based on principal but I could have married you three months ago."

He moved his arm from around her shoulder, reached into his pocket, and pulled out a small, velvet box. He took out a two-carat diamond engagement ring and placed it on her finger.

"Gina, will you make a covenant with me and God and become my wife, my friend, my lover, bone of my bone and flesh of my flesh? Let's turn this world upside down for Jesus. I love you. I loved you in the spirit before I even met you in the flesh. Will you marry me?"

Gina paused and looked at the ring. Then she looked up at Bishop. "Please, Gina, say something."

"Wow. This is beautiful, Tony. Yes, I will marry you. I would have married you three months ago if you had asked."

"You mean you would have said yes?"

"Yes. I would have. I would love to be your wife, your friend your lover, bone of your bone, flesh of your flesh. Let's turn this world upside down for Jesus."

He embraced her and gently kissed her lips. With the excitement of the moment, his hands started to tremble as he touched Gina's cheeks.

"Let's elope! I'm a preacher. I can marry us. Hey, you're a preacher. You can marry us." They laughed.

"Elope? Tony, you are just kidding, right?

"Yes. I guess. But it is not good for me to touch or caress your soft body. I cannot handle it. Believe me, I cannot. Let's go

129

back to the car." Bishop put his hands back into his pocket and took some slow, deep breaths.

"Okay, so is this a good time to set a date, Tony?

"The sooner the better. I have waited for you a long time and I don't want to mess up the blessings of the Lord by becoming intimate with you before you are truly mine. So however long it takes for you to find a dress is long enough."

"Okay, okay. I get the picture. Thank you for waiting for me."

"You are welcome. You are worth waiting for."

Chapter 16

The Guilt of The Past

Many people gathered for the engagement celebration.

"Congratulation to you both," said Elder and Sister Robinson. "You two make a fine couple."

"Thank you. Please pray for us," Bishop said.

They talked with the Robinsons a few more minutes and then Gina excused herself to the ladies room.

"Hurry back, dear. "I want you to meet my cousin and his wife."

"Okay. Give me a few minutes," she said.

"Okay baby, I love you."

"I love you too."

The ladies room was large and eloquent. The lounge area was beautifully decorated and the stalls and sinks were spacious. As Gina gets ready to exit one of the stalls, she overheard three women from the church talking about her and Bishop.

"I can't believe Bishop is going to marry her. He waited all these years for her while she married some sinner that nearly killed her."

"Girl, I can't believe it either. Now you know she ain't right."

"Yeah, she got just what she deserved; calling herself some preacher and being unequally yoked with that man."

"Well, I sure hope Bishop knows what he is doing because God has plenty of pure virgins he could have. He doesn't have to marry some devil's leftovers."

"Exactly! He has a high position and he shouldn't marry just any old thing."

The women walked out of the bathroom without even realizing Gina's presence. Gina began to weep as she stared at herself in the mirror. The enemy began to fight her mind as she lashed out at herself in the mirror.

"Yeah, you don't deserve him, Gina. Because of you, he had to wait all these years. Look at all you've missed and worse, you've wasted his life and yours. You don't deserve him. Why don't you just leave and go back to the United States? You would be better off. Don't mess up the Bishop's reputation by marrying him."

Gina cleaned her face, left the bathroom, and returned to her seat beside Bishop who took her hand and introduced her to his cousin and his wife.

"This is my wife to be - Gina. Gina, this is my cousin, Elder Graham, and Monica, his wife."

As the couples greeted each other, the three sisters who had been in the bathroom with Gina walked by, rolling their eyes and shaking their heads.

"Gina, are you okay," Bishop asked.

"Yes, I am fine. I was just thinking about how blessed I am to have you in my life."

"You are a blessing in my life, Gina."

For the rest of the evening, Gina continued to rehearse in her mind the things she overheard in the bathroom. She could hardly wait to get home. The devil continued to fight her mind. *"I bet everyone here is thinking the same thing. You don't even deserve the Bishop."*

For an entire week, Gina battled in her mind the guilt of her past and decided to call off the wedding and return to the United States. The night before leaving for the airport, she wrote a letter to Bishop explaining her decision.

Tony, by the time you read this letter I will be on a plane headed back to the United States. I don't deserve you. If I did, I would have made the right choice years ago. I would have met you at that church service the night you came for me. I messed up both of our lives. I am sorry to have been so foolish. Please forgive me. You deserve better and your church deserves better.

Her letter was short and to the point. She put it with her purse and planned to leave it on her door for Bishop to find when he came over to get her for their morning walk. Gina awoke at 5 a.m. and began to pack for her trip home. Meanwhile, Bishop Smith was awakened from a deep sleep by an angel. "Wake up, Tony, wake up. Gina is under strong demonic attack. You must go to her now. She needs you."

Bishop rubbed his eyes and looked at the clock. It was 6 a.m. He thought to himself, "Gina should be asleep but okay, Lord. I will call her."

When he did not get an answer, he got dressed and drove to her home, praying and interceding for Gina. Gina put the note on her door and loaded her suitcase into the trunk of a taxi. As she reached into her purse, the plane ticket fell to the ground. Gina hopped into the taxi, which sped away to the airport. About 10 minutes later, Bishop arrived at her home. He pulled the note off the front door and began to read it.

"Oh no, oh no," he shouted in disbelief. He then noticed the plane ticket on the ground. He picked it up and drove as fast as he could to the airport.

"Lord please don't let this woman leave me. What happened, Lord?"

God answered in a calm voice, "The enemy has lied to her and you must tell her the truth."

Bishop continued to drive fast. He prayed all the way there.

"Lord, when she sees her ticket is missing, she will probably just buy another one. Lord, please hold that plane. It's almost seven now and departure time is 8:45. God I know you can do exceedingly and abundantly above all I can ask or think so I ask you to allow me to see her before she gets on that plane. Just let me see her Lord. Man, I don't believe this devil. A week before my wedding and he is still throwing darts. Satan you are a liar. Loose Gina now in the name of Jesus!"

When he pulled up to the airport, he parked his car and quickly ran toward the building. Just then, he noticed Gina standing at the check-in counter looking in her purse. Gasping for breath he ran over to her and handed her the plane ticket.

"Are you looking for this?"

"Yes, I am. How did you get it?"

"You must have dropped it while you were getting into the car or something. Gina, why are you leaving me?"

"Tony, you were not supposed to know until I was gone. Why are you up so early?"

"The Lord woke me up and told me that you needed me."

"Oh, he did?"

"Yes. And I am here for you, baby. I don't know what has happened but I am here for you. Tell me why do you think you need to go back to the United States?"

"Because I don't deserve you."

Gina couldn't hold back the tears any longer. She cried uncontrollably.

"I messed up so bad and I can't forgive myself. If I was all that how did I miss God and marry a devil? I missed my Boaz and ended up in a horrible pit. I can't trust myself. Who knows what else I will mess up in the spirit? I will just sit under my pastor and be fed the Word. I am giving up ministry and going back home. I do not know how I could let the enemy blind me like that; and then to expect you to just forget about how I held up our lives. Tony, you can't forget what I have done. All the things I am dealing with right now are just too much."

"Gina, where is all this coming from? My heart is looking forward to our future not your or my mistakes of the past. Your burden is heavy because God didn't put it on you. His yoke is easy and His burden is light. What is going on? I've noticed you have been acting different since the engagement party. Did something happen that I am not aware of?"

Gina shared in detail what she overheard the three sisters say in the ladies room.

"Gina, I'm sorry. I knew something happened to you."

He began to encourage her.

"Can't you see this is a tactic of Satan to stop our wedding and the ministry God has placed in us? Gina, don't be so hard on yourself. I will not allow you to judge yourself this way." Tony gently touches both of Gina's shoulders and pulls her close to him. God does not judge you like this so why are you? He knew your choices before He created you and He had grace and mercy to sustain you. Even in your most difficult time, God was there to sustain you. Do not spend another moment looking back on what you can't change. Today is a new day. You now have a chance to help someone else; to help them see how God can take a mistake and turn it into a miracle. Here we are in Africa, one week from getting married, delayed but not denied. Yes, we both have been through some storms and some loneliness. But God's promise to me is that I would have you as my wife and to Him be the glory, the honor, and the praise. I refuse to give the devil any praise. This is the week of our wedding. Can't you see that this is the devil's last shot to keep us apart? Don't let him win, Gina. Don't let him win. We have power over him. I speak to your spirit to be encouraged. Be lifted, Gina. Shake off this doubt and unbelief. I don't want any other woman on this earth. I don't care what those women said. I don't care if they have 50,000 virgins for me to choose from. I don't want a one. I only want you." Tony embraced Gina. "Please don't leave. I have waited so long for you. Please see that this is the enemy. Let's talk. Better yet, let's pray."

As Gina wiped the tears from her eyes, Bishop's name was paged over the intercom.

"Anthony Smith, please come to the information desk. You have an urgent phone call."

"Gina my cell phone is broken and I told Elder Brunson to page me at the airport if there were any emergencies."

Final call for Flight 227, the announcer continued.

"Look, Gina, I am going to the desk to get this call. All I am asking you is to be here when I get back. We can buy another plane ticket if need be. I just want to pray with you. Let's seek God first, that's all."

"Okay, I won't get on the plane. I promise. I will stay here to pray with you."

He looked at her and lovingly held her face in his hands.

"You promise?"

"I promise. Now go get your phone call."

"Okay. I will be right back." He kissed her lips quickly and briskly walked to the phone to receive the call from Elder Brunson.

"Bishop, this is Elder Brunson. We just received tragic news concerning three of our members. Sister Jenny, Sister Mia, and Sister Wanda were in a serious car accident and not one of them is expected to survive. They are in the emergency room now."

Bishop walked back toward the gate and began to pray within himself.

"Lord, what am I going to do? Please direct me. Gina has been hurt and is about to leave me and now three of my faithful members are near death. God help me."

When he got back to the area where Gina was standing, she was nowhere to be found and her plane was taxiing to the runway. He grabbed his head and closed his eyes for a moment to hold back the tears. He took a deep breath and said to himself, "God, she didn't wait. She promised she would wait for me. Lord, I can't get on a plane and follow her. Not now."

Just then he looked over and saw Gina sitting in a chair and resting her chin in her hands as if she was praying. She looked up and invited him to come pray with her.

"Come on. Let's call on the name of the Lord. We need to pull down some strongholds."

He thought to himself. "Thank God she's still here."
He said to her, "I thought you had left me. I have to sit down and let my heart rate go down. Look, Gina, I know that we have to pray about our relationship and work some things out but there is an emergency and I have to go to the hospital. Three of my members were in a tragic accident and are near death. I really need to go and pray for them. I know that God has blessed you in the ministry of

healing and even resurrecting the dead. Sister Jenny, Sister Mia, and Sister Wanda are very important to me and have been a great support of my ministry. I have to be there for them."

Gina looked at Bishop and thought back on the three women who were talking in the bathroom. These were the same women who talked about her and now they are facing death.

"Sure, I will go and touch and agree with you. We know that with God, nothing shall be impossible."

"By the way, who were the women that you overheard talking about you and that discouraged you? Whoever they are, they were mightily used by the enemy. And don't tell me you can't reveal it because you can. This is serious. This is our future we are talking about here. The snares of people's mouths were used in an attempt to tear us apart."

"Bishop, Tony, I will tell you later but right now let's concentrate on these three souls that are in need of a miracle."

She grabbed his hand and said, "Let's go. We can get my luggage later."

As they drove to the hospital in Bishop's car, they continued to talk.

"You know what, Gina? I am blessed to know a woman of your caliber. You are such an anointed woman. You are caring and giving to others. Here we are on the way to the hospital and you could have easily said that you needed to get your luggage to be sure your things were okay. But you denied your own needs to see about someone else's. That's one of the many reasons why I love you so much, Gina. I never ever thought I could love someone again after my wife died. But God has answered all my prayers and more by sending you in my life."

He reached for her hand and gently held it has he drove. "Let's pray for our relationship now as I drive."

"Ok. Let's pray."

The two prayed together and the glory of the Lord overshadowed the car. God confirmed that it is His will for them to marry. God spoke to Gina's spirit saying 'I love you, my daughter, you are forgiven. Now do my will as I have asked. Preach my word and love your husband.'

Chapter 17
Love Never Fails

When they arrived at the hospital, Elder Brunson informed Bishop Smith that Camille was already dead and that Mia and Wanda were in critical condition. Bishop looked at Gina and said, "Well, woman of God. Let's go raise the dead first."

"Let's." she said.

They walk down the hall side by side quietly praying in the Holy Ghost. As they entered the room, Camille's mother was crying loudly over Camille's body.

"Jesus, oh Jesus. My baby, my baby. Oh Lord help me," she cried.

Bishop walked closer to the bed and announced, "Anyone in here who does not believe that Jesus is the resurrection and the life must leave now."

Everyone stood at attention but no one left the room. Bishop began to pray. "Camille, come forth! Death, loose your hold!"

Gina touched Camille's forehead and began to pray and speak life to her. "Life to you my sister. In the name of Jesus, arise."

Camille moved her mouth and took deep breaths. Her eyes opened and she spoke. "Oh! Oh, God. Oh, God. I am sorry. Forgive me, Lord. I am sorry."

She looked up and saw everyone gathered in the room Gina, Bishop Smith, her family. "God is so merciful. He gave me a second chance. Lord, I thank you. I will serve you, Lord."

Camille looked at Gina and Bishop Smith standing over her and began to weep and cry. Gina touched Camille on her shoulder.

"It's ok Camille. We love you. Get some rest."

Gina and Bishop Smith left the room praising God for the miracle they had just witnessed.

Doctors, nurses, and the hospital staff were shocked to hear that a dead woman had come back to life. Also, by the power of prayer, Mia and Wanda fully recovered and were ready to be discharged from the hospital in just three days.

Gina told Tony that Mia, Wanda, and Camille were the three women that she overheard speaking in the bathroom. Tony was surprised that the women would say such things but even more surprised of Gina's display of Godly character.

"It had to be God enabling you Gina, to give you the ability and faith to pray for those who had hurt you. They were obviously used by the enemy to keep us apart."

Tony embraced Gina and again thanked God for her being in his life.

"Woman you are so precious, loving, forgiving, and your works speak of your relationship with God. I am so blessed to be able to Love you and to share my life with you. You are staying in my life and you are going to be my wife. Correct?"

Gina looked into his eyes and she was speechless.

Two years later, Bishop Smith was standing behind the pulpit giving remarks at his pastor's appreciation service.

"Giving honor to God who is the author and the finisher of our faith. Without Him we are nothing. We have had some good days and some bad days. We have experienced loss, persecutions, and sufferings. At some points in my life, I wondered when my weeping would end and be replaced with joy. Some of the attacks have come from within my own mind and other attacks have come from the enemy or through vessels he has used. Nevertheless, I will not complain. Romans 8:18 says 'For I reckon that the sufferings of this present time are not worthy to be compared with the glory which shall be revealed in us.' You see, God did not promise that we would go through this life without trouble or opposition. As a matter of fact, Jesus said just the opposite in St. John 16:33 which says, 'These things I have spoken unto you, that in me ye might have peace. In the world ye shall have tribulation: but be of good cheer; I have overcome the world.' To help us live in peace even if everything around us is chaotic, Jesus reminds us that the Father loves us and that He was going to be with the Father. He wants His children to know that we are loved and if we are convinced in our own hearts that God loves us just the way we are, then we can accomplish great things for the Kingdom, ourselves, and others. Look at your neighbor and say be persuaded in your own heart that God loves you."

The congregation repeated Bishop's words to each other.

"On a side note now... don't misunderstand my point. Just because we are loved doesn't mean we are without a need to repent, change, or improve. God's love will always be with us and our actions don't change that fact. For the Bible says in Romans 5:8, 'But God commendeth his love toward us, in that, while we were yet sinners, Christ died for us.' Yes God loves His people and He also expects us to live a holy and a separated life from the ungodly practices of the world. So my point is that when we are sincere and walking in love, whatever we ask in Jesus' name, He will do, that the Father may be glorified in the Son. It's all about God's glory and His will. If in your heart you have purposed to love God and others and serve God with every ounce of your being, He will do whatever you ask. That's the word according to St. John 14. So be of good cheer. Jesus has overcome this world and so can you."

Bishop continued his remarks.

"In my conclusion, it is because of God's peace and overcoming power that I stand here today. I am thankful to Him for the power that He has given all of us and for His plans for our lives. I appreciate how God can orchestrate our lives and position us to be in a certain place, city, or country, at a particular time in order to fulfill His purpose. Can we explain every valley, every hardship, or every attack? No, we can't. But one thing is for sure. We can believe that God loves us and He showed us by giving His life on the cross of Calvary and shedding His blood. And with God's love, we can recover from any obstacle that comes our way. As we celebrate my years in ministry, I am not holding up my life wondering why? God, why did my wife die of cancer and I was left alone to manage a ministry? To be transparent, I asked God why, but I didn't stop living. Keep living church. Keep serving God. We will understand things better by and by."

He began to bring his words of encouragement to a close.

"Job did not know why he suffered such great loss in one day. He lost his children, his wealth, his health, and support systems. God asked Satan in Job 1:8, "Hast thou considered my servant Job, that there is none like him in the earth, a perfect and an upright man, one that fears God, and shuns evil?' Job had no idea that Satan challenged God asking, 'Does Job fear God for nothing? But put forth thine hand now, and touch all that he hath, and he will curse thee to thy face.' Some things you go through are because the enemy hates your praise and despises your relationship with God. The enemy wants to prove that you are in it for the money, a title, position, family name, or personal gain and that you would curse God if your world became uncomfortable or heavy with turmoil. God, on one hand, is saying that you are His servant and you will love Him no matter what happens in your life. You will bless His

144

name and keep His commandments in the secret places where no one sees what you are doing and in the public's view. And on the other hand, Satan is trying to kill, steal, and destroy you through any person or entity available. He hopes that you, too, will curse God and reject the precious gospel of Jesus Christ of which we are blessed to be partakers. All I have to say, children of the most high God, is pass your tests and prove the devil wrong. Declare I will serve Jesus 'til the day I die. As a soldier in the army of the Lord, it is my reasonable service. I will praise Him through persecutions and abuse. I will praise him in sickness and in health. I will praise Him when I'm broke and when I am rich. I will praise Him when I am single and when I am married. In everything give thanks for this is the will of God in Christ Jesus concerning you. Halleluiah! If I lose everything, I will still praise Him because I brought nothing with me when I was born and I surely can't take anything with me when I die. The salvation of the soul is first priority so if you lose friends, family, money, titles, your health, or material things during this life, but still hold on to this great salvation, you have profited more than enough. For what profit has a man to gain the whole world and lose his soul? Give glory to God if you are saved, blood washed, filled with His spirit, and your name is written in heaven! Somebody ought to give God the praise."

He lifted his hands in praise. And the congregation praised the Lord with him. After the congregation had finished dancing and praising God, Bishop Smith continued to speak.

"We have to get out of here because I was supposed to give remarks, not preach," he laughed. "But I just want to thank God for my wife and son He has blessed me with. Many of you know of the miracle of how I met this lovely woman of God and the tragedies she and I both have endured in life. We made it through those storms

145

by the grace of God. Will you all put your hands together as my lovely wife comes forth? Gina please come up here with me and greet the saints; and bring Tony, Jr., too."

The congregation clapped and praised God as Gina walked down the aisles. Bishop continued to talk.

"Gina is a survivor. God has spared this woman from death, delivered her from a satanic attack, self-hatred, and rejection. She is a powerful woman of God that serves the Lord faithfully. She doesn't just have a testimony, she is a testimony. God gave me just what I needed when I needed it. I love you, Gina."

Applause and praises continued to fill the church as did camera flashes.

"Bishop," someone yelled from the congregation, asking to get a close-up shot of the family. With the glory of the Lord shining upon Gina's face, she walked on stage with her husband and waved to the congregation.

"Praise the Lord. God is good and His mercy endures forever! I love you too, Tony."

The two shared a kiss on the cheek as Bishop helped Gina up the steps.

"Amen, amen. Gina, stand here for the picture and I'll hold Tony, Jr."

They smiled at the camera as the congregation cheered and yelled out how much they loved the pastor and his family.

"We love you guys."

"We love you, Bishop."

"We love you, Evangelist Gina."

"God bless you!"

"Look this way, Tony, Jr., and smile"

Bishop and Gina embraced their son together, thinking in their hearts that it was nobody but Jesus who had brought them this far.

.

Afterword

Oh My God! I Married A Devil challenges the reader to take an honest look at relationships and domestic abuse. It is written to evoke, inspire, and encourage anyone who has been in a bad relationship. More specifically, it examines when 'bad' becomes abuse. Anyone who has been in an abusive relationship or impacted by domestic abuse will find something to relate to in this story.

Diana designed this book to be used as an empowerment tool, to give the reader hope, peace, and eventually joy! Scripture tells us that God desires us to be happy and healthy. His desire for us is that our minds, our bodies, even our relationships be healthy and whole. 2 Timothy 1:7 tells us, "For God has not given us a spirit of fear, but of power and of love and of a sound mind" (NKJV).

Each year in October, the nation strives to raise awareness about the important issue of domestic violence. Domestic violence is the willful intimidation, physical assault, battery, sexual assault, and/or other abusive behavior perpetrated by an intimate partner against another. It is an epidemic affecting individuals in every community, regardless of age, economic status, race, religion, nationality, educational background, or gender. Domestic violence is often accompanied by emotionally abusive and controlling behavior, and thus is part of a systematic pattern of dominance and control that could result in physical injury, psychological trauma, and sometimes death. The consequences of domestic violence can cross generations and truly last a lifetime.

As an active board member for Sistercare Inc., I know the struggle of domestic violence in all communities. In South Carolina where Diana resides, the Attorney General's office notes that more than 36,000 victims report a domestic violence incident to law enforcement across the state each year. According to a report released by the Violence Policy Center in Washington D.C., South Carolina has moved in the wrong direction in a national ranking on criminal domestic violence deaths—first in the United States in the number of women killed by men. The homicide rate among females murdered by males was 2.54 per 100,000 people. It is the third time South Carolina has been ranked number one. In 2011, South Carolina ranked second.

In that same Violence Policy Center report, nationwide 1,707 females were murdered by males in single victim/single offender incidents in 2011, at a rate of 1.17 per 100,000. For homicides in which the victim to offender relationship could be identified, 94 percent of female victims were murdered by a male they knew. Sixteen times as many females were murdered by a male they knew (1,509 victims) than were killed by male strangers (92 victims). Among victims who knew their offenders, 61 percent of female homicide victims were wives or intimate acquaintances of their killers. In 87 percent of all incidents where the circumstances could be determined, the homicides were not related to the commission of any other felony, such as rape or robbery.

Statistics like these indicate we have a long way to go in getting the message out about domestic violence. Therefore, we must continue to do so by any means necessary. That is why I applaud Diana for using her gift as a writer and author of this fiction to help raise awareness about the horrors of domestic violence. If you've read *Oh My God! I Married A Devil.* I believe it will help you to better assess, evaluate, and even value your own relationships!

Antjuan O. Seawright

Antjuan O. Seawright is president and CEO of Sunrise Communications in Columbia, South Carolina and has served on the board of Sistercare, Inc. since 2009. Sistercare, Inc. provides community counseling, community education and awareness, court advocacy, emergency shelters, a 24-Hour Service Telephone Line, a Shelter Follow-Up Program, transitional housing, and Hispanic outreach services for battered women and their children throughout the Midlands of South Carolina.

Stay Connected

151

Host a reading group or Bible study. Suggested topics of discussion include:

- Single and waiting
- Important characteristics of a potential mate
- Warning signs to look for when dating
- Listening to God's voice
- Walking in obedience
- Submitting to leadership
- The power of prayer
- How to control anger
- Overcoming Domestic Violence
- How to make wise choices
- Patience
- Self-love and forgiveness
- God's unconditional love
- The sacrifice of praise

Contact Diana Morris at
dmministries1@gmail
www.dianalmorris.com

Made in the USA
Columbia, SC
10 October 2022

69259915R00098